365
REASONS TO BE
PROUD TO BE
IRISH

RICHARD HAPPER

365
REASONS TO BE
PROUD TO BE
IRISH

MAGICAL MOMENTS IN IRELAND'S HISTORY

PORTICO

To Rachel, a fine colleen if ever there was one.

First published in the United Kingdom in 2014 by
Portico Books
10 Southcombe Street
London
W14 0RA

An imprint of Anova Books Company Ltd

Illustrations by Lindsey Spinks

ISBN 978 1 90939 640 1

A CIP catalogue record for this book is available from the British Library.

10 9 8 7 6 5 4 3 2 1

Printed and bound by Toppan Leefung Printing Limited, China

This book can be ordered direct from the publisher at
www.anovabooks.com

'This is one race of people for whom psychoanalysis is of no use whatsoever.'

Sigmund Freud, on the Irish

INTRODUCTION

So what is it that makes you proud to be Irish?

The chances are it's not the shamrocks and the leprechauns and the mountain dew and the colleens and the blarney and all that shite.

It could be the fact that Ireland has produced writers of the calibre of James Joyce and Oscar Wilde, explorers as brave as Ernest Shackleton, actors as good as Peter O'Toole, bands as famous as U2, beer as ubiquitous as Guinness.

Maybe it's the world-changing inventions: the hypodermic needle, the Beaufort scale, the submarine, the lighthouse, the dollar sign and, most importantly of all, the cream cracker.

But to those who really know and love this country it's probably the mad, self-contradictory, only-in-bloody-Ireland stuff that makes your heart swell: the fact that the nation that can pass the world's first animal welfare laws can also invent the harpoon gun; how we can fight to the death over a peaceful religion, but all get behind the boxer Barry McGuigan; that Ireland was the first country to ban smoking in the workplace, and the site of the world's largest tobacco factory; how for years contraception was illegal and yet we make the world's supplies of Viagra.

It doesn't make sense. Not one bloody bit of it. From the north to the south, from the east to the west, this is a land of oddballs, gobshites, gowls, feeks and plain old drunks.

But, by God, doesn't it make you proud? Every day of the year.

'In Ireland the inevitable never happens and the unexpected constantly occurs.'

Rev. Sir John Pentland Mahaffy

JANUARY

LOOK AT THE NECK ON THAT GIRL

1 Trust an Irish girl to blarney her way to the front of the biggest queue in the world. Over 12 million immigrants passed through the famous Ellis Island facility in New York harbour and the very first of them was Annie Moore from Co. Cork, who arrived today in 1892, on what was her 15th birthday. History says she was travelling with her two younger brothers to meet her parents, who were already in New York, but she probably just thought it was a nightclub doing cheap drinks. As the first person through the newly opened facility, she was proudly presented with a $10 gold piece, which her Da took right off her.

LOVING LIFE

Many an Irishman thinks he has such a gift of the gab that he can talk any colleen into bed. But you'd have to go a long way to beat Frank Harris. This randy bugger from Galway turned shagging into an art form with his legendary book *My Life and Loves* (published in Paris today in 1922). This graphic account of Harris's sexual adventures also dished the dirty on the celebrities of his day. Instantly banned in his homeland, the first volume was burnt by customs officials and the second got him charged with corrupting public morals. It didn't hurt sales that Harris chose to illustrate the book with many, many pictures of nude women.

IN SPACE NO ONE CAN HEAR AN IRISHMAN SCREAM

Who did all the work in *Star Trek*? Captain Kirk? Spock? Jean-Luc Picard? Don't be daft: it was Miles O'Brien, played by Ireland's own Colm Meaney. He starred in 216 episodes of *Star Trek: The Next Generation* and *Star Trek: Deep Space Nine* (which first aired today in 1993), the second highest tally of any actor in the show. O'Brien is often deliberately placed under considerable pressure in storylines – the production team called these 'O'Brien-must-suffer' episodes. Why they chose an Irishman for this honour is a mystery.

HOLEY MOBY

Blowing whales out of the water is generally frowned upon these days, but not so in 1760. Back then the prevailing opinion was that the blubbery bastards deserved everything they got. Which is why Thomas Nesbitt from Donegal invented the harpoon gun, which he first used on this day. Mounted on a swivel, his gun was amazingly accurate, and Nesbitt got so good that for many years he didn't miss a single whale. Mind you, they do make a pretty big target.

QUACKS ON TOUR

During the Franco-Prussian war a large group of Irish medical volunteers embarked for France. Organised as the *Ambulance Irlandais*, they collected wounded soldiers from the battlefields, returning them to the Irish casualty station where doctors treated their wounds and operated if necessary. The Irish Ambulance left for home with their heads held high today in 1871, having earned the gratitude of the soldiers and the respect of the local people. Their venture was one of the first of its kind anywhere, and became a template for later volunteering programmes.

A STORMING IDEA

 The most savage storm in 300 years ripped across Ireland today in 1839, obliterating at least 20 per cent of the houses in Dublin. Not much to be proud of there, you might think. However, this being Ireland, some genius managed to find a bright side to this utter disaster. The tempest inspired the Director of Armagh Observatory, the Reverend Romney Robinson, to develop the cup-anemometer, or wind-measuring device. Rev. Robinson's design is still whirling proudly today.

A STRONG CUP OF JOE

 As with most things in Ireland, the weather played a major part in what happened on this night in 1943. A late flight departed from Shannon for Newfoundland but turned back in filthy weather. Airport staff were dragged from their beds and head chef Joe Sheridan was told to prepare 'something warm' for the freezing passengers. He simply poured a generous dose of whiskey into their coffees. Thanking him for the wonderful drink, one of them asked Joe if he used Brazilian Coffee. Joe jokingly answered, 'No that was Irish Coffee!'

NOTHING COMPARES TO HER

A beautiful Irish girl, shorn of her hair and any adornment, stares straight at you as she sings a song that moves her to tears. The video for Sinead O'Connor's stripped-back, heart-rending take on a Prince album track was nothing less than a landmark cultural moment. After its release today in 1990, it was played heavily on MTV, propelling the ever-controversial O'Connor to stardom and immortalising her iconic image.

HE SLEPT ON THE PROBLEM

The way the frame of his Triumph motorcycle twisted on fast corners unsettled Rex McCandless from Co. Down (which is fair enough). So he decided to do something about it and invented the legendary 'featherbed' motorbike frame – so-called because that's what it felt like you were riding. It was patented today in 1952. Stronger and more rigid, this design was adopted by the Norton Motorcycle Company, who dominated the sport for decades and broke many world speed records. The featherbed still shapes bikes today.

TATTOO YOU

10 If you've ever woken up with the name of a barely remembered lover etched into your skin, you can thank Irishman Samuel O'Reilly. After emigrating to New York, O'Reilly became a tattooist with an eye for the future of body art. In 1891, he adapted an electric pen designed by Thomas Edison into the first modern tattooing machine, with the same basic needle, tube and ink reservoir that devices use today. He first demonstrated it on this day, and the visionary O'Reilly was probably disappointed when his first customer wanted only the word 'Mammy' and a big anchor on his arm.

THE INCREDIBLE KAVANAGH

Considering how he started in life, Arthur Kavanagh achieved more than any other Irishman – in fact, more than most people. Born in Co. Carlow without legs and only the stumps of arms, Kavanagh decided to bloody well get on with things. He trained himself to ride using his stumps to hold the reins, and became an expert angler and a good painter. He travelled across Asia and today in 1851 he shot his first tiger. He later became an MP and a Privy Councillor. Totally unselfconscious, on visiting Abbeyleix, Co. Laois, he once said, 'It's an extraordinary thing, I haven't been here for five years, but the station master recognised me!'

PARK LIFE

Phoenix Park isn't just a nice place for a sit-down with the paper and a cheese roll. Its 6¾ mile (11km) wall encloses 1,747 acres (707ha), making it the world's largest municipal park. There's room for cricket and polo fields, Ashtown Castle, the residences of the Irish President and the US Ambassador, as well as Garda (Irish police) HQ and the world's third oldest zoo (not the same thing). It started life as a very private piece of royal hunting land. But soon after the Earl of Chesterfield's appointment as Lord Lieutenant of Ireland, today in 1745, he decided to let in the *hoi polloi*, cheese rolls and all.

BEAUFORT BLOWS INTO HISTORY

It's fitting that the man who created the scale for measuring how bloody windy it is should be an Irishman. Commander Francis Beaufort made his name in the British Navy, but he was born in Navan, Co. Meath. He realised that sailors needed a standard measure of bad weather – what was a hurricane to one man was a mere zephyr to an old tar. Launched today in 1806, Beaufort's original scale had 14 categories, running from 0 (calm) to 13 (totally fecking howling).

THE MODEL HERO

Thomas Lefroy, of Carrigglas Manor near Longford, Co. Longford, was a brilliant Trinity College scholar who became an MP, Privy Councillor and Lord Chief Justice. But his true fame lies in a fictitious world – he was the model for Mr Darcy in Jane Austen's *Pride and Prejudice*. Austen visited his house several times when she stayed in the area, and found him intoxicatingly attractive. After meeting him today in 1796 she wrote to a friend that the two of them had indulged in behaviour 'most profligate and shocking'. The courtship ultimately fizzled out, but soon afterwards she produced her most famous book.

THE WORLD ACCORDING TO SLOANE

 The British Museum is perhaps the world's finest collection of cultural and historic artefacts, and it first opened today in 1759. Of course, the whole thing only came into being thanks to an Irishman, Sir Hans Sloane. A famous physician and scientist, he bequeathed his immense collection of personal antiquities to found the museum. He also gave his name to Sloane Square in London and to Sir Hans Sloane Square in his birthplace, Killyleagh, Co. Down.

THE HERO'S HERO

 There's tough, and then there's Ernest Shackleton. Born in Co. Kildare, the famous explorer led the Antarctic expedition that today in 1909 reached the South Magnetic Pole. In 1914 he tried to cross Antarctica, but his ship *Endurance* was crushed by ice. Shackleton led a 932-mile (1,500km) voyage in an open boat across savage seas to find help for his stranded comrades. All survived. Shackleton once gave his daily ration, a single biscuit, to a sick colleague, who wrote in his diary: 'All the money that was ever minted would not have bought that biscuit and the remembrance of that sacrifice will never leave me.'

BYRONIC BROTH

 It's an indisputable fact that in Ireland everyone's mammy makes the best Irish stew on the planet. Its blend of mutton, spuds, onions and parsley just hits the spot when the west wind brings the rain in sideways. And of course she has her own magic ingredient, a tradition that goes right back to the dish's first mention in print. This was today in 1814 in a satire by the poet Byron: 'The Devil...dined on...a rebel or so in an Irish stew.' Sounds a bit chewy, mind you.

POCKRICH'S 1ST SYMPHONY IN WINE FLAT MINOR

 If anyone was going to invent a musical instrument based on drink containers, it was going to be an Irishman. Step forward Richard Pockrich, who in 1741 perfected the art of playing an array of wine glasses filled with different amounts of liquid by stroking their rims. First seen in public on this day, his virtuoso performances on the 'musical glasses', also known as the glass harp, became known throughout Europe, the public responding well to an instrument that actually necessitated boozing for its use.

SOGGY MOGGY

Aviation history was made today in 1785 when Richard Crosbie became Ireland's first aeronaut, flying across Dublin below a hydrogen balloon, just 14 months after the Montgolfier brothers in France. However, although Crosbie wasn't the very first human balloonist, his cat was certainly the first feline aviator. To test his contraption, Crosbie had earlier launched his intrepid puss heavenwards only to see the wind veer sharply towards the north-east. The balloon was later seen speeding gaily over the west coast of Scotland, before ditching in the sea near the Isle of Man. Happily, the heroic cat was rescued by a passing fisherman.

LANE LEAVES A LASTING IMPRESSION

It's fair to say that many early 20th-century art critics thought Impressionist paintings were a load of blotchy bollocks. Hugh Lane, however, spotted the genius on the canvas. The art dealer from Co. Cork collected masterpieces by Manet, Monet, Degas, Renoir and Morisot among others, and then donated his collection to found Dublin's Municipal Gallery of Modern Art today in 1908. This was the first public gallery of modern art anywhere in the world.

THE HIGHER SPIRE

 The Spire of Dublin is a stainless steel, spike-like monument that shoots 397½ ft (121.2m) up from the middle of O'Connell Street. As well as reflecting the light in a rather beautiful way, it is also the tallest sculpture in the world. Completed today in 2003, it is officially called the Monument of Light, but locally it is affectionately known as 'The Stiletto in the Ghetto'.

WATER HERO

 Western Australia owes much of its prosperity to Charles Yelverton O'Connor from Co. Meath. Engineers in the 19th century thought building a harbour at Fremantle would be impossible due to sand shoals and a limestone bar at the river mouth. 'CY' proved them wrong, building an elegant and capacious port. He then turned to an even stiffer problem – how to transport water for 350 miles (563km), uphill, from Mundaring Weir to the growing goldfields of Kalgoorlie. His solution was the Goldfields Water Supply scheme – the world's longest water main. It was turned on today in 1903, and still supplies 100,000 people with 5 million gallons (22,730,450l) of water daily.

THIS MIGHT SMART A LITTLE

If you've ever had an endoscopy this one may make you wince. Today in 1865, Dr Francis Cruise first used his revolutionary new endoscope. This device allowed the Dublin doctor to boldly go where no man had gone before and diagnose diseases of the bladder in living patients, and perform internal operations. His invention used mirrors and a lamp fuelled by petroleum and camphor, and it did have a tendency to get a little warm. Ouch.

HEEL GO FAR

The story goes that Humphrey O'Sullivan from Skibbereen, Co. Cork was so sick of getting sore feet from standing in his print shop all day that he started to stand on a small rubber mat. When colleagues kept nicking it he cut two pieces out of the rubber mat and tacked them to his shoes. Realising that there might be something in this he then patented his invention – the rubber heel – today in 1899. It's a great tale, but it kind of begs the question, why didn't he just get a chair like a normal person?

THE PRESSURE OF A GAS IS PROPORTIONAL TO THE...?

That the pressure and volume of a gas are inversely proportional is more than just a formula that is half-remembered by millions of schoolchildren every year – it's a law that made constructing steam and internal combustion engines possible. And it was worked out by Robert Boyle, who was born today, in 1627, at Lismore Castle, Co. Waterford. Boyle was a brilliant experimenter who is now regarded as one of the founders of modern chemistry, and a pioneer of scientific method, even if, as an alchemist, he undertook many of his experiments with the objective of turning lead into gold.

BAD HEALTH GOES UP IN SMOKE

Ireland was the first country in the world to introduce a smoking ban in workplaces when the act passed today in 2004. There was a 10 per cent drop in heart attacks in the first year alone, among many other health benefits. Of course, the number of grumpy-looking smokers standing outside pubs in the rain has risen exponentially, but you can't win them all.

SHOW ME THE MUMMY

27 For generations of young visitors to Belfast's Ulster Museum, Takabuti has been one of its captivating – and scary – exhibits. It is also a very important historic artefact. When it was first unveiled today in 1835, Takabuti was one of the first mummies in the world to be seen outside Egypt. Scholars deciphered her hieroglyphs to learn that Takabuti was a married woman, 20–30 years old and the mistress of a rich house in Thebes, now called Luxor. Her coffin dates to 660 BC, making Takabuti nearly 3,000 years old. She's looking good on it.

THE BUCK STARTS HERE

28 Even by the standards of hell-raising 18th-century Irish aristocrats, Buck Whaley was proudly in a class of his own. He once lost £14,000 in a single night at a Paris casino. He also bet £25,000 that he could travel to Jerusalem and return safely (the city was then part of the Ottoman Empire and full of wild bandits). Cheered by dockside crowds, Whaley charmed his way through Europe and arrived today in 1789. He then played handball against the walls of Jerusalem, stayed for a month and returned to claim his money, although he had spent almost as much *en route*.

A SHOCKING DISCOVERY

29 We take limitless electricity for granted, and that's partly thanks to the inventive spark of Father Nicholas Callan. This holy man was also Professor of Physics at Maynooth College, Co. Kildare, and today in 1836 he tested the first induction coil. The forerunner of today's transformers, coils were vital in X-ray machines, early radio transmitters, and arc lighting. Callan measured his voltages by shocking his students. One lad named William Walsh, who later became Archbishop of Dublin, was rendered unconscious. The College ordered Callan to be more careful, so he started electrocuting turkeys instead.

CHOP CHOP, MAN, WE HAVEN'T GOT ALL DAY

 Today in 1649, the unpopular King Charles I had his head snicked off in London. However, decapitating the monarch was such a touchy issue that no English executioner was prepared to do it. In the end, they had to recruit a headsman from Ireland, where, curiously, there seemed to be less of a shortage of men willing to chop an English king's head off. In the end the fun – sorry, duty – fell to a man named Gunning from Galway, who by all accounts did a smart job of it.

SIGN OF THE DIMES

It's only fitting that a rich man should invent the US dollar sign, but it might be surprising to discover he came from Coleraine, Co. Londonderry. Oliver Pollock emigrated to the US and became a wealthy merchant and Governor of Louisiana. He financed many American operations during the revolutionary war, often dealing with the Spanish, and therefore in pesos. In his numerous transactions he used the standard abbreviation for pesos – a large P with a small s above it to the right. Over time this was simplified to just the upright stroke of the P running through the s – hence $. His new symbol was first published in an accountancy textbook today in 1797.

FEBRUARY

AN IRISHMAN WALKS INTO A TAVERN...

Johannes Scotus Eriugena was a 9th-century Irish theologian who was one of the most accomplished scholars in Europe. He wrote and translated many important works and his image graced the new £5 note when it was issued today in 1976. But he is perhaps best remembered for coining the world's first 'drunk Irishman' joke. When asked by the French king, Charles the Bald, 'What separates a drunkard from an Irishman?', Eriugena replied, 'Only a table.'

UN-PICKUPABLE

Perhaps the most brilliant writer the world has ever known, James Joyce was born today in 1882 in Dublin. On the same day in 1922, he published his masterpiece, *Ulysses*. This was clearly a work of genius, even if it did make everyone else feel a bit inadequate, frankly. *Ulysses* also goes down in history as the book that is most started-but-never-finished. Not many people know that Joyce was keraunophobic – an aunt told him at an impressionable age that thunderstorms were a sign of God's wrath.

PILLARS OF THE COMMUNITY

Just because it's a bank, doesn't mean it can't be a good thing. The Bank of Ireland on College Green in Dublin was originally built as the Irish Houses of Parliament (its foundation laid today in 1729), and was the world's first purpose-built, two-chamber parliament building. The design, by Edward Lovett Pearce, is a masterpiece of Palladian architecture that was imitated by the British Museum and US Capitol building. After the Act of Union the building was for a time a garrison, an art gallery and then... that other thing.

SURVIVAL OF THE FATTEST

 You may know that it was on a voyage of discovery to the Galapagos Islands that Charles Darwin came up with the idea for evolution by natural selection. But he wasn't the first ever human resident of the archipelago – that honour goes to Irish sailor Patrick Watkins, who was marooned on the island Floreana today in 1807. Alas, Watkins merely ate the local wildlife rather than studying it, so missing out on greater historical fame.

BLOODY BRILLIANT

 Everyone has heard of Bram Stoker, but the writer who put a lot of bite in the vampire genre was another Irishman, Sheridan Le Fanu from Chapelizod, Dublin. He staked out a terrific reputation as an author of mysterious and macabre fiction and his novel *Uncle Silas* (1864) is a masterpiece of gothic horror. But it was his tale *Carmilla* (published today in 1872), about a lesbian vampire in central Europe that really wowed Bram Stoker and inspired his writing of *Dracula* 25 years later.

O'BRIEN'S SLAM DUNK

As great big lanky buggers go, Patrick Cotter O'Brien was the biggest and lankiest of the lot. Born in 1760 in Kinsale, Co. Cork, O'Brien was known as the 'Irish Giant' and he spent much of his life on the sideshow circuit. Today in 1972 his remains were examined and he was found to have stood 2.46m (8ft 1in) tall. He was the first person in history to be confirmed at over 243.8cm (8ft) tall and remains only one of 13 people worldwide to reach that height. Damn shame basketball wasn't invented until 1891.

SUB-STANDARD DESIGNS

Today the US Navy has 71 sleek submarines, but its very first such vessel was built by John Holland, an engineer from Liscannor, Co. Clare. The modestly named USS *Holland* was the first submarine in the world that could actually go any decent distance underwater. Today in 1899 Holland formed a company to build them, and soon Holland had also built the first Royal Navy submarine, called – guess what? – the *Holland 1*. He later invented an apparatus that helped sailors escape from damaged submarines, which was pretty useful considering how dodgy these early underwater tin cans looked.

SPREADING THE WEALTH

The Cork Butter Market opened on this day in 1770 and soon became the world's largest butter market. Butter was carefully categorised into five types and then shipped to waiting pieces of bread all over the world. Irish butter grew famous for its quality and we were its biggest exporter. This might sound like a homely trade, but it's easy to understand and you can see where the actual money came from, unlike some economic miracles we can think of.

HE FELT THE EARTH MOVE

Robert Mallet blasted himself into science textbooks by using dynamite to measure the speed of waves in rocks. Born in Dublin, Mallet used his findings to help prepare his (literally) groundbreaking paper 'On the Dynamics of Earthquakes', which he presented to the Royal Irish Academy today in 1846. This paper pretty much founded the modern science of seismology, a term that Mallet himself coined. He also came up with 'epicentre'. Before getting into earthquakes, Mallet helped make the famous iron railings that surround Trinity College.

WE'RE CRACKERS ABOUT BISCUITS

What would grannies do without cream crackers? Cheese's best friend was invented by Joseph Haughton in his Dublin home, and then first manufactured by the city's Jacob's bakery on this day in 1885. The name comes from the way the mixture is creamed during manufacture. We can also be proud that crackers are, officially, the hardest biscuit in the world to eat quickly. The world record for eating three is a surprising 34.78 seconds. It's really not easy – have a crack!

EYE DON'T WANT TO LOOK

Eye operations must have been absolutely terrifying to undergo in 1750, but after Sylvester O'Halloran published his then-definitive work on how to sort out glaucoma (we don't want to think about exactly how that was done), they were at least a bit dig-and-hope-for-the-best. O'Halloran had many outstanding achievements, including co-founding the Limerick County Infirmary and the Royal College of Surgeons in Ireland, today in 1784. This has since become one of the world's most respected medical training establishments. He was also an expert on Gaelic poetry.

AN IDEA THAT GOT UNDER HIS SKIN

Dr Francis Rynd was working at Dublin's Meath Hospital for the poor in 1844 when he realised that the best way to get pain-relieving drugs into a patient would be through a hollow needle inserted directly into the bloodstream. This was considered impossible at the time. But, in those days before such inconvenient things as research or medical trials, Rynd simply gave it a stab. He developed a needle and injected a solution of morphia in creosote (!) into patients, publishing his results today in 1845. Now we use around 15 billion hypodermic syringes every year.

THINK I'LL TRY GREYHOUNDS NEXT

Very few people stand head and shoulders above others in their field, but racehorse trainer Vincent O'Brien was certainly one of them. He started out training National Hunt horses and went on to bag four Cheltenham Gold Cups, and in 1955 won his third Grand National in a row, a feat that remains unsurpassed. Aged 41 he decided he needed a new challenge, so he focused on flat racing and went on to train six Epsom Derby winners. He won 1,529 races in Ireland alone, and was champion Irish trainer 13 times. Today, in 2003, he was voted the greatest influence in horse-racing history, if only for making more people jealous than any one else.

VALENTINE'S VENUE

Feeling passionate? Then head to Whitefriar Street in Dublin. Valentine, the patron saint of engaged couples and happy marriages (obviously not the same thing) died on this day AD 269 in Rome and was laid to rest there. But in 1836, Father John Spratt, an Irish priest, gave such an impressive sermon in Rome that Pope Gregory XVI gave him Valentine's remains. Spratt placed the reliquary in Whitefriar Street Church where it lies still. Spratt also got a letter confirming the relics really were those of St. Valentine signed by the Pope, so it must be true.

BIGGER REALLY IS BETTER

William Parsons was a passionate amateur astronomer who also happened to be the Earl of Rosse and stinking rich. So he built the world's largest telescope, the 72in (183cm) Leviathan, in his back garden at Birr Castle, C. Offaly. Parsons had to build his own foundry to cast two 3½ ton metal mirrors (he needed a spare for when the damp climate dulled the one in use) and a 70ft (21.3m) high stone building to hold the thing. From its first use today in 1845, this monster wasn't surpassed in size for 70 years, and was so powerful it was the first telescope to show that nebulae are masses of stars.

MITCHELL SEES THE LIGHT

Building a lighthouse on sandy or muddy sea floors was a problem that had foxed engineers until Dublin-born Alexander Mitchell came up with the brilliant idea of using screw piles. His method was simple, cheap and allowed strong lighthouses and ship moorings to be sunk in deep water and on shifting sands. His first screw-pile lighthouse was lit today in 1841 and the design was soon employed with great success all over the world. This invention is all the more impressive when you consider that Mitchell was blind.

MILES AHEAD OF THE PACK

Eamonn Coghlan from Drimnagh in Dublin was one of the most brilliantly consistent middle-distance runners the world has ever seen. His unprecedented success on indoor running tracks included winning 52 of his 70 races at 1500m and 1 mile from 1974 to 1987. The world indoor mile record that he set today in 1983 stood for 14 years and is still the second fastest of all time. As many of the indoor tracks were in those days wooden, Coghlan was waggishly nicknamed 'The Chairman of the Boards'. After retiring he became the first man over 40 years old to run a sub-four-minute mile.

SO BAD THEY WERE BRILLIANT

It takes a special sort of talent to be so shite at things that you actually set records at it. Today in 2004 saw Northern Ireland become European Champions of not scoring a soccer goal. They had played ten goalless games on the bounce. Then on 18 February 2004, in a friendly against Norway, and to ironic cheers from the strangely still-loyal crowd, they finally ended the drought when David Healy headed the ball home. The lads didn't let that success change them though – they still lost 4–1.

TREE-MENDOUS RESULT

Children have dared each other to climb it, romances have blossomed in its shade and who knows what secrets the majestic King Oak at Charleville, Co. Offaly, has had whispered into its bark. This mysterious giant tree is around 800 years old, with mighty lower branches stretching 164ft (50m). Today in 2013 it was chosen as one of the European Trees of the Year. The judges have obviously forgiven the oak its murderous past – an ancient legend said that if a branch should fall, a death in the Bury family (the owners of the Charleville estate) would ensue. In 1963 the tree was hit by a thunderbolt and Charles Howard Bury died only a few weeks later...

ART FOR ART'S SAKE

20 As a watercolour painter, Frederic Burton from Corofin, Co. Clare earned high praise in his lifetime (he was knighted) and after it (his *Meeting on the Turret Stairs* was voted Ireland's favourite painting in 2012). But it was as director of London's National Gallery that his artistic passion really flourished. Today in 1874 he began an unprecedented programme of art collection on behalf of the gallery. He bought over 500 works, many of them masterpieces by Botticelli, Canaletto, van Dyck and Leonardo da Vinci, creating possibly the finest art collection in the world.

OUR FRATERNAL SISTER

 Freemasons aren't known for their sexual equality, which is what makes Irish girl Elizabeth St Leger so unusual. She is the only woman ever initiated into the cult – sorry, Brethren. Elizabeth fell asleep in the winter darkness of this evening in 1710, in the library next to where the local Lodge was meeting. The house was being renovated, and she watched the secret shenanigans through a gap in the wall. Dislodging a brick, she was discovered, and fainted. The Lodge decided the best way to ensure her silence was to initiate her when she awoke, which they duly, and uniquely, did.

HE THOUGHT IT WOOD LAST FOREVER

At one time the 'kyanising' method of preserving wood was seen as nothing short of world-changing. It amazed the scientists of the day, and the mighty Michael Faraday even made it the subject of his inaugural lecture at the Royal Institution of Great Britain today in 1833. This application of bichloride of mercury to wood was invented by John Kyan from Dublin. The method was eventually replaced by cheaper creosote, but if you're ever in Regent's Park, London, take a look at the wooden palings – they're still in great nick, nearly 180 years after they were treated.

CENTRAL LOCATION, COMES WITH OWN POLICEMAN

For all Ireland's run-ins with the British government in Downing Street, London over the years, it's kind of ironic that the road itself was named after an Irishman. George Downing left his native Dublin for success in the New World. He was in the first graduating class of nine students at Harvard, and became a crafty diplomat who served both Cromwell and Charles II. He managed to wrangle the city of New York from the Dutch and his political efforts earned him a valuable piece of London land. Today, in 1664, he got permission to build the street that bears his name.

IT'S A BIT HOT IN HERE, DON'T YOU THINK?

Richard Brinsley Sheridan was a famous writer and wit, whose plays such as *The Rivals* and *The School for Scandal* were hugely popular in his day and are still being performed and adapted for film in the 21st century. The Dublin native also found time to be a Member of Parliament, fight a couple of duels and own the most famous theatre in London – the Theatre Royal, Drury Lane. This burned down today in 1809, but Sheridan was even witty about that – seen by a friend drinking a glass of wine in the street while watching the fire, Sheridan famously said, 'A man may surely be allowed to take a glass of wine by his own fireside.'

FOUR MOORE

Our efforts in the soccer World Cup have been a mixed bag, but today in 1934 one of our boys achieved something special. While playing against Belgium in a qualifying match at Dalymount Park, Dublin, Shamrock Rovers' Paddy Moore became the first person in history to score four goals in a World Cup game. Alas the 11 players of Belgium also managed four between them, and the match finished a 4–4 draw.

SORRY, I'M RESTING THIS YEAR. AND NEXT

Irish passport-holder Daniel Day Lewis won his third Academy Award for Best Actor today in 2012, an achievement no other actor has ever accomplished. He is one of the most selective actors in the film industry, starring in just five films since 1998. Hang on a minute – 'selective'? For most of us, only doing five jobs in 15 years would get you slapped with the description 'lazy feckin' beggar'.

COLD COMFORT

You trek thousands of miles in a frozen, featureless wilderness, discover a new country and everyone remembers you for finding a dead guy. Such is the lot of Francis M'Clintock from Dundalk, Co. Louth. From 1852 to 1854, M'Clintock travelled 1,400 miles (2,253km) in the Canadian Arctic by man-hauled sled and discovered 800 miles (1,287km) of previously unknown coastline. He later led a mission to find the missing explorer Sir John Franklin, organised by Franklin's wife. Today in 1859 he found the vital clues to his compatriot's disappearance – Franklin was a goner. This was bad news to bring back, but M'Clintock still got a knighthood.

DRUMM FINDS INVENTING EASY-PEASY

Where would we be without rechargeable batteries? Probably not walking into each other while staring at our phones. Still, it's worth being proud of Co. Down chemist Dr James Drumm, who invented the nickel-zinc rechargeable battery, and today in 1932 used it to power a train the 80 miles (129km) from Inchicore to Portarlington and back on a single charge. This served the Dublin–Bray line for 16 years. Perhaps equally usefully, Drumm devised a way to can peas so that they stayed green; before that they had turned a rather uninviting grey.

MARCH

NOT CONTENT TO BE A SPECTATOR

1 Media moguls are nothing new – Richard Steele from Dublin was a major one back in the 18th century. He published the first *Tatler* magazine and the original *Spectator* (first issue today in 1711). This was the most phenomenally popular magazine of its time, with an estimated 60,000 people – 10 per cent of the population – reading it in London alone. This was an incredible figure considering only 50 per cent could read. He also founded the first *Guardian* newspaper.

SECOND TO NONE

'Feed a fever' sounds like a phrase grannies invented. But really it was Irish doctor Robert Graves, and it was revolutionary at the time. He introduced practical medical training and co-founded the *Dublin Journal of Medical Science* today in 1832. Graves was also the first to time the pulse by watch – in fact he invented the whole concept of the second hand on watches, without bothering to patent it. Graves was so good at languages that he was once imprisoned as a German spy in Austria for travelling without a passport – the authorities couldn't believe that an Irishman could speak their language so well.

SICK OF THE CITY

Every day Dublin's O'Connell Street attracts shoppers, tourists and workers to pace past its elegant buildings, while every night it draws the drunks to puke all over it. But it's not just a vital part of Dublin – it's also the widest urban street in Europe, which is hard to believe when you can't dodge the spew. Originally called Sackville Street, it took its current moniker today in 1924. Oddly, O'Connell Bridge is one of the few in the world that is wider than it is long.

LITTLE MAN WITH BIG IDEAS

Leprechauns – mystical, magical man-fairy or load of tourist-oriented shite? Well, they really do exist, at least according to David Jones from Lisburn, Co. Antrim/Co. Down – he was one. Jones stood just 2ft 2in (29cm) and proclaimed himself the 'Living Leprechaun'. Rather than fixing shoes while cackling and shinning down rainbows, Jones dealt with littleness by putting a lawnmower engine into a child's pedal car. From today in 1960 he was a regular sight as he drove about town, presumably nearly getting flattened on every outing.

LYNCH'S REVOLUTION

The image of bearded, long-haired revolutionary Che Guevara wearing a beret and staring hard into the future has become a global symbol of rebellion. That image was popularised in a red and black poster produced by Irish artist Jim Fitzpatrick, from a picture taken by Alberto Korda, today in 1960. Fitzpatrick had been an admirer ever since Che had walked into the bar of the Marine Hotel in Kilkee, Co. Clare, where Fitzpatrick was working, with two Cubans and ordered an Irish whiskey. (Guevara was stopping over at Shannon *en route* from Moscow to Cuba.) Fittingly, Guevara's true surname was Lynch, as his father was of Irish descent.

YE OLDE CHIP WRAPPER

The oldest copy of the *Belfast News Letter* still in existence is from today in 1738, but it began life as a simple one- or two-page letter the year before. The paper had already been around for decades when it carried news of the American Declaration of Independence. This makes the *Belfast News Letter* the world's oldest English-language newspaper to be continuously published. Whether or not it has been continuously worth reading is another issue entirely.

FISH AND CHIPS

Thanks to its semiconductor production facilities, Leixlip, Co. Kildare is one of the most technologically advanced places in the world. More importantly, it is also the site of the world's first hydraulic fish lift. When a hydroelectric plant threatened the passage of salmon, a unique lift was opened for them today in 1951. The homeward-bound fish swim through gates into a canal-like lock, which is then closed behind them. The basin is flooded and the top gates opened to allow the leaping lovelies to progress upstream to where they can be hoiked out of the water by anglers.

BUILT TO LAST

It seems that Irish farmers have been getting stuck in bogs longer than any other. As you make your way down the breezy Mayo coast, you might think that the ditches and low mounds you pass near Ballycastle belong to just another old farm. But these are the Céide fields, which date back 5,500 years, making them the world's oldest field systems. This complex of walls, houses and tombs is protected beneath a bog and is the largest Stone Age site on the planet. And the top-notch Irish building standards are maintained even now – the visitor centre won a prestigious architectural award today in 1994.

FREEDOM OF MISINFORMATION

It's baffling why the US National Security Agency would want to secretly tap into everyone's pictures of their drunken mates on Facebook, but it seems they really are doing it. So we might all soon be turning to Freenet, the communication platform that is censorship-resistant. This tool for digital freedom was developed by Ian Clarke from Navan, Co. Meath, and first released today in 2000. It uses encryption and secondary computers to store data anonymously. So now we can send each other cute cat pictures without interference from an evil foreign government.

BROWN'S TOWN

10 Next time you're strolling round downtown Buenos Aires, make your way to the leafy square named Plaza Almirante Brown – it's named after William Brown from Foxford, Co. Mayo. This brilliant seaman escaped the clutches of the British Navy (after being press-ganged by them) and created the Argentine Navy, becoming its first commander. Today in 1814 he led the new nation's maritime forces into battle for the first time. He went on to win many famous victories and is one of Argentina's national heroes – there are actually more than 1,200 streets named after him.

LIKE WATCHING GRASS GROW

11 The Botanic Gardens in Belfast are more than just a fine place to relax with a slab of Harp (even though you're not really allowed to) – they're home to the historic Palm House conservatory. Completed in 1840, this is one of the first and finest curved cast-iron glasshouses in the world, pre-dating the ones at Kew in London. The Palm House was specially designed to house very tall plants, such as the 36ft (11m) tall Globe Spear Lily, which finally started to bloom today in 2005 after 23 years doing nothing. In Victorian times the glasshouse attracted 10,000 visitors every Saturday. Well, there was no TV then.

MARCH

CABLE-KNIT TV

 Talk about a big break. The Clancy Brothers and Tommy Makem did Ireland proud tonight in 1961 when they performed on *The Ed Sullivan Show* for 16 minutes for a television audience of 80 million people. This famous folk-music moment had an inspirational influence on a watching Bob Dylan but, more importantly, pretty much created the Aran sweater industry overnight.

THIS'LL LEARN YA

 Founded today in 1592 as the 'mother' of a new university, Trinity College, Dublin is certainly a grand old dame. It's one of the world's great academic institutions, and one of its most beautiful. The list of alumni is a *Who's Who* of Irish greats in art and science: Jonathan Swift, Bram Stoker, Oscar Wilde, Samuel Beckett and Ernest Walton, among many. Another glory is the library, which holds five million printed volumes including some of the most important books in world literature, such as the *Book of Kells*. It's also home to the Brian Boru harp, the symbol of Ireland, and is one of six libraries in Britain and Ireland that is legally entitled to a copy of every book published, including this one. We are honoured.

GOD'S OWN GROUND

Croke Park has seen many record-breaking moments on its holy turf (officially holy – it was named after Archbishop Thomas Croke, one of the first patron's of the Gaelic Athletic Association (GAA). But the place itself is also remarkable. When it was reopened after its redevelopment today in 2005, its capacity of 82,300 made it the largest non-soccer stadium in Europe, and the fourth largest of any sort. And in 2009, the 82,208 crowd at the Heineken Cup rugby semi-final, in which Leinster defeated Munster 25–6, was a new world record for a club rugby union game.

HE STOOPED TO CONQUER

When your student career at Trinity is more notable for the riot you start in the Marshalsea debtor's prison, observers might think you won't go very far. But Oliver Goldsmith became a world-famous Irish playwright and also, variously, an apothecary, gambler, busker and poet. He became very famous for his novel *The Vicar of Wakefield* and a play, *She Stoops to Conquer*, which was first performed on this night in 1773. Ironically, for a man who was a chronic gambler, drinker and spendthrift, he coined the phrase 'goody two-shoes'.

THE SMALL TOWN WITH
THE BIG-NAME BISHOP

16 When Pope Francis gave his first audience in Rome today in 2013, he really ought to have been with his flock in Kilfenora, Co. Clare. That's because the Pope is technically the bishop of the parish. This quirk is unique in the world and stems from the diocese being joined with one in Galway in 1750, only for a Papal Dictate of 1883 to rule that no bishop can work in two provinces, thereby leaving Kilfenora in the capable hands of His Holiness.

I MIGHT JUST HAVE A QUIET
ONE THIS YEAR

17 Today we are proud to celebrate the feast day of St Gertrude of Nivelles, patron saint of travellers, gardeners and cats – just kidding, you know what day this is! Curiously, St Patrick was originally British, but he was captured by Irish pirates and grew up here. He later became a bishop and worked tirelessly to spread Christianity throughout Ireland. Nowadays we commemorate his sacrifice and piety by wearing leprechaun hats and getting absolutely legless.

DUTY-FREE TAKES OFF

Conveniently located at the edge of the Atlantic, Shannon Airport became famous in the years after the Second World War as the most popular transatlantic gateway for flights between Europe and the US. And lovers of cheap booze (which is most of us) can also be proud that today in 1947 Shannon became the first airport in the world to offer duty-free shopping.

ACHTUNG DOLLY

It's all very well rewarding the Irish people we're proud of, but things went a bit far today in 2000. Rock maestro Bono was given the freedom of the city of Dublin and this ancient honour came with certain rights – one of which was the right to pasture sheep on St Stephen's Green in the centre of the city. His Rockness duly exercised this right, to the consternation of park-goers and the ire of the groundsman. Surely the man can afford a field or two of his own?

'THERE'S NO BAD PUBLICITY EXCEPT AN OBITUARY'

As the 'drinker with a writing problem', Brendan Behan was one of the best-loved Irishmen of his time. Hired by Guinness to write an advertising slogan, Behan was paid upfront (with half a dozen kegs) and spent the next month getting to know the product. The sum of his efforts: 'Guinness makes you drunk' was at least accurate. Equally pithy were his last words, spoken on this day in 1964 to the nuns standing over his bed, 'God bless you, may your sons all be bishops.'

THIS MEETING WILL COME TO ORDER (ITS DRINKS)

Whether it's a noble gathering of like-minded knowledge lovers or simply a great way to get your mates together for a piss-up, the student society has a long history. And in Dublin it's longer than anywhere else. The College Historical Society of Trinity College (the 'Hist') had its first meeting today in 1770, making it the oldest in the world. Since then it has had many famous members, including Bram Stoker, Wolfe Tone and Oscar Wilde.

RUBY'S HOTTEST PLATTERS

If you looked at the music chart today in 1955 you would see that a full quarter of the hit records were by one singer – Ruby Murray from Belfast. The chart was a top 20 then, and Ruby had five hit singles on it – not reissues, nor old record companies cashing in on a current success, but five genuine new songs. This was, and remains, a record. Of course, we can also be very proud of Ruby for giving her name to the rhyming slang for everyone's favourite takeaway food.

PETER SOCKS IT TO THEM

After famously being rejected by the Abbey Theatre's drama school in Dublin because he couldn't speak Irish, Peter O'Toole from Connemara went on to do all right for himself as an actor. He got his big break playing the lead in the 1962 film *Lawrence of Arabia*, a performance voted number one in a poll of the 100 Greatest Performances of All Time. Although he is the most nominated actor never actually to win an Oscar (a total of eight), today in 2003 he picked up an honorary one. Proud of his Irish ancestry, O'Toole always wears a green item of clothing, most often a sock.

NOCTURNE ALLY

If it weren't for Irishman John Field, the music of Frédéric Chopin, Johannes Brahms, Robert Schumann and Franz Liszt would have been very different. Born in Dublin to a musical family, Field gave his first public performance today in 1792, at the tender age of nine. He found fame in London before moving to Russia in 1802. It was here that he originated the piano nocturne, the mood-evoking form that was made famous by Chopin and so admired by other classical composers.

HE WENT OUT IN STYLE

Turlough O'Carolan was one of the greatest-ever harp players and the composer of over 220 Irish songs, and has a fair claim to being Ireland's national composer. A supremely gifted musician, he was so popular that weddings and funerals were often delayed until he got there to perform. Old Turlough was a noted lover of whiskey, women and song who went out of this life as he lived it. His final composition was to the butler who brought his last drink, today in 1738, and the wake that followed his death lasted for four days.

NOT SO RUN-OF-THE-MILL

26 Far from being just another twee Irish woollen outlet shop, Avoca Handweavers in Co. Wicklow is actually one of the world's oldest manufacturing companies. The mill on the banks of the chuckling River Avoca started spinning in 1723, and this historic institution was saved today in 1974 by the man sent to close it down – solicitor Donald Pratt. Since then it has become famous for its high-quality throws, blankets and clothes. Its grounds are also home to several very rare trees, which are just right for sitting under – presumably on a nice woollen rug.

ASLAN'S LAND

27 The much-loved *Chronicles of Narnia* sprouted from the brain of Belfast-born academic Clive Staples (CS) Lewis. He completed the first tale, *The Lion, the Witch and the Wardrobe*, today in 1949, and since then the seven books have shifted over 100 million copies in 47 languages. Although Lewis took the name 'Narnia' from Narni in Italy, the inspiration for the magical land itself was the Mourne Mountains, which Lewis roamed as a child and which presumably had more fauns, ice queens and talking lions in them than they do now.

DO YOU REMEMBER WHEN WE USED TO SING?

It's the fourth most requested song of all time, a favourite of George W. Bush and Bill Clinton, and no wedding is complete without a drunken auntie falling over in the chorus – 'Brown Eyed Girl' by Van Morrison was recorded today in 1967. Although it's his most famous tune and everyone else loves it, it's one of the Belfast singer's least-favourite compositions. Is this because as an artist he never looks back, or could it be because, thanks to a nasty contract, he gets no royalties from it?

THE BETTER SETTER

We've even invented dogs. Well, the Irish Setter at least was bred here – the breed standard was first drawn up by the Irish Red Setter Club in Dublin today in 1886. This noble pooch has a remarkable nose to find and track game birds, a keen disposition for the hunt, and long legs to avoid the many, many bogs that he would doubtless find himself traipsing through. Considering the setter is so fast, friendly and reliable it's interesting that transport company Bus Éireann chose it as their logo.

THE CHAMP LEAVES THE FIELD BEHIND

 Not many people are allowed to carry off a cool nickname, but then there's no one like jockey Anthony Peter McCoy from Co. Antrim. Sometimes known as Tony, usually people just call him 'The Champ'. Here's why: he rode his first in 1992 aged just 17 and went on to bag 3,863 more (as of today in 2013). This is more than any other National Hunt jockey ever, by miles. McCoy has been Champion Jockey every year he has been professional – that's 18 titles in a row. The previous record was seven. In 2010 he was voted BBC Sports Personality of the Year, the first time a jockey had won. Not content with breaking records, he has also broken almost every bone in his body, some of them multiple times.

BELFAST'S TITANIC AMBITION

 When RMS *Titanic* sank in the North Atlantic with the loss of 1,500 souls it was one of the world's worst peacetime disasters. Today in 1909, Harland and Wolff of Belfast laid down what would be the largest, most luxurious ship afloat. At 882ft (269m) long she was almost the length of three football pitches: even the gantry needed to build the vessel dwarfed Belfast's buildings; and she used as much steel as the Eiffel tower. When she was launched down the River Lagan she carried the romantic hopes of an era with her.

APRIL

TOP OF THE DOCKS

When the White Star Line shipping company dreamed up the biggest ships in the world, the Olympic-class liners, they realised they needed an even bigger dock to put them in. So they excavated 8,122,400 cu. ft (230,000m³) of clay (enough to fill London's Albert Hall) and built the Thomson Graving Dock. At 879ft (268m) long and 44ft (13.4m) deep, it was the largest in the world when it opened today in 1911. It cost more than Belfast City Hall and its pumps could shift its 21 million gallons (95,467,890l) in 100 minutes – that's two swimming pools every minute. Amazingly, it was still in everyday use in the late 1980s.

RED RUM GALLOPS INTO HISTORY

Probably the most famous racehorse of all time, Red Rum, was bred at Rossenarra stud in Kells, Co. Kilkenny. His name came from the last three letters of his dam (Mared) and sire (Quorum) respectively. 'Rummy' won the Grand National in 1973 for the first time from an incredible 30 lengths back, won it again in 1974, came second in the next two years and triumphed for an unprecedented third time today in 1977. It's one of those rare records that is so special it's unlikely ever to be broken.

RAINDROPS STOP FALLING ON MY DEAD

Today in 1938 it stopped raining in Limerick. Of course that's not unusual in itself, but this time the rain stayed away – for 37 days. This was magic at first – we could show the world that our weather wasn't always misty or raining or bloody drizzling. It was the longest drought ever recorded in the country. Then a wise soul pointed out that if there was a shortage of water, there would be a shortage of things made from water. Breath was collectively sucked in, the local Father had a word with the man upstairs, and on 10 May it blessedly started lashing it down again.

JUST DON'T BURN THE PADDLE

 The *Sirius* usually worked the Cork–London postal route, but today in 1838 she slipped out of Cobh, Co. Cork, and headed west. The small Irish paddle steamer arrived in New York 18 days later, the first ship to cross the Atlantic under steam power alone. Coal had run so low on the crossing that the crew burned cabin furniture, spare yards and one mast. *Sirius* beat the much bigger and faster *Great Western* – the largest passenger ship in the world – to the honour by just a few hours.

EVERYBODY GET OUT AND BLOW

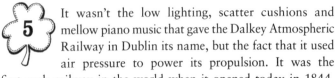 It wasn't the low lighting, scatter cushions and mellow piano music that gave the Dalkey Atmospheric Railway in Dublin its name, but the fact that it used air pressure to power its propulsion. It was the first such railway in the world when it opened today in 1844. Imaginative as it was, the railway wasn't that practical – starting from Kingstown, the train required pushing by hand until the piston engaged with the tube. But it operated for ten years and was an influence on the great Isambard Kingdom Brunel, who built a similar railway in England three years after visiting Dalkey.

GREEN MIGHT HAVE BEEN NICER

Trust an Irishman to be the first person to paint the town red. Today in 1837, Henry Beresford, Marquess of Waterford, and some aristocratic pals arrived at Melton Mowbray tollgate, England, after a refreshing day at Croxton races. The toll keeper asked for payment, the boys refused and, seizing some ladders and pots of red paint being used for gatehouse repairs, proceeded to paint the man. They then rampaged into town, painting a pub, the post office, the Leicestershire banking company and a policeman. The next day a new phrase entered the language, and the Marquess entered prison.

A CROSS TO BEAR

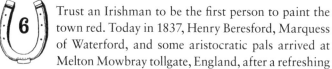

A favourite exhibit in Dublin's National Museum is the 12th century Cross of Cong. This processional cross and reliquary is exquisitely ornamented with gold, silver and precious stones. The Cross of Cong is not just extraordinarily beautiful; it is one of the finest examples of medieval metalwork in Western Europe. Furthermore, to believers, the fragment of wood it contains is a relic of the True Cross, on which Jesus was crucified today in AD 30.

APRIL

I REMEMBER WHEN ALL THIS WAS FIELDS

Samuel McCaughey from Tullynewey was a farmer's son who decided to try his luck in Australia. He landed in Melbourne today in 1856, and to save money he walked the 200 miles (322km) to his uncle's property. His thriftiness, hard work and genial Irish humour helped him build a flourishing business. After buying numerous neighbouring farms, his holding was the largest farm in history. At over 3 million acres (1,214,000ha), it was larger than Northern Ireland.

COMIC BOOK HERO

It only takes one look at the cinema listings to see we're living in an age when comic books are kicking the asses of other forms of entertainment. One man who has helped the comic's meteoric rise in recent years is Garth Ennis of Holywood, Co. Down. Ennis earned his writing spurs on the classic *2000 AD*, penning the title's flagship character, Judge Dredd. He then created the fearlessly original *Preacher*, which debuted today in 1995 and was rated by many as one of the greatest comics of all time. British newspaper *The Guardian* even voted a *Preacher* collection its Book of the Week.

IT WAS HIS WIFE'S PROBLEM, REALLY

When William Molyneux's wife went blind, the Irish scientist turned her misfortune into one of the great philosophical questions, 'Molyneux's Problem': 'If a person born blind can feel the differences between shapes such as spheres and cubes, could he distinguish those objects by sight if given the ability to see?' The mightiest minds debated this thorny problem of sense and existentialism for centuries until today, in 2011, when a professor at Massachusetts Institute of Technology in Boston published the results of a study in which he had cured five patients of their congenital blindness. The answer is 'no'.

SHIPS 'R' US

Two up-and-coming engineers called Edward and Gustav formed a partnership in Belfast today in 1861. There was something a bit special about these boys and their company would go on to produce some of the most famous ships the world has ever known, including the *Titanic*. They built over 2,000 vessels and, with up to 40,000 employees, pretty much defined the growth of the city. Of course, they were better known by their surnames, Harland and Wolff.

ATLANTIC CROSSING

 His first attempt to fly the Atlantic only got 300 miles (483km) off the coast of Co. Kerry. But Dublin-born James Fitzmaurice was a trier, and his second effort, today in 1928, fared a lot better. With two other crew members, his German Junkers W33 took off from Baldonnel Aerodrome, Dublin, and landed 36½ hours later at Greenly Island in Quebec, Canada. It was the first ever flight across the Atlantic from east to west.

SOUL MUSIC

 The music in Dublin's Temple Bar may now be mostly tonally challenged buskers' renditions of 'Whiskey in the Jar', but today in 1742 it was a whole lot classier. Fishamble Street hosted the world premiere performance of Handel's 'Messiah', sung by the choirs of St Patrick's and Christ Church Dublin. The audience was enraptured, and one Dublin clergyman was so overcome by soloist Susanna Cibber's rendering of 'He was despised' that he leapt to his feet and yelled: 'Woman, for this be all thy sins forgiven thee!'

HE'S ONLY DOING IT TO GET A REACTION

The atom (well, a few of them, actually) was first split today in 1932 by the Irish physicist Ernest Walton and his English colleague John Cockcroft. Their 600,000-volt particle accelerator shot protons into lithium atoms, producing alpha particles and energy. This reaction was the first experimental proof of Einstein's $E=mc^2$ and the dawn of the nuclear age. Whether that's a good thing or an utter frigging disaster is open to debate. But it did earn Walton Ireland's only Nobel Prize for a science in 1951.

HIS CAREER WENT INTO EXTRA TIME

With soccer players seeming to retire ever earlier these days, goalkeeper Pat Jennings from Co. Down set records that'll take a lot of beating. He made his international debut today in 1964, the same day George Best made his. After 119 games and 22 years, he had his last game in the 1986 World Cup – on his 41st birthday. He was then the oldest player to appear in the competition and had made the most international appearances ever. He still holds the Northern Ireland caps record. He also famously scored a goal from his own area in the 1967 Charity Shield.

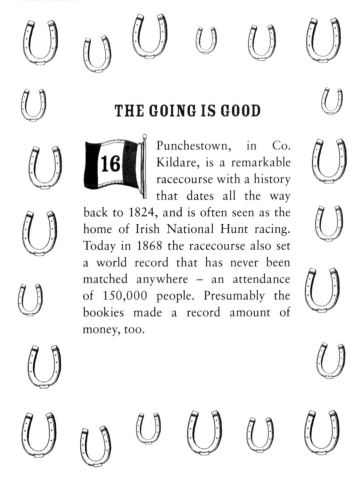

THE GOING IS GOOD

Punchestown, in Co. Kildare, is a remarkable racecourse with a history that dates all the way back to 1824, and is often seen as the home of Irish National Hunt racing. Today in 1868 the racecourse also set a world record that has never been matched anywhere – an attendance of 150,000 people. Presumably the bookies made a record amount of money, too.

HOLYWOOD, NOT HOLLYWOOD

Imagine a building big enough to paint the world's largest ocean liners. That vast shed, at Harland & Wolff's Belfast shipyard, is now one of Europe's biggest film studios – The Paint Hall. Some major movies have come to life here, including the 2008 sci-fi adventure film *City of Ember* and the medieval comedy *Your Highness*. It's also famously the home of the hugely popular TV series *Game of Thrones* (which premiered today in 2011). Many of the show's exterior scenes are also shot in Ireland. Those nude scenes must have been bloody chilly.

STROKE CITY

Whether you call it Derry, Londonderry or the modern mouthful of Derry/Londonderry, you're still talking about one of the finest walled cities in the world. The fortifications were built in the 17th century, making it the last walled town to be built in Europe and now the most complete and spectacular. Derry is also one of the few cities in Europe that never saw its fortifications breached, withstanding several sieges. The last one started today in 1689 and the defences remained unpenetrated for 105 days. Some local wag consequently gave it the nickname 'The Maiden City'.

APRIL

HIS REPUTATION WAS INTACT

'The James Joyce of structural engineering' is how Peter Rice from Dundalk, Co. Louth, is known, and his ingenuity made possible some of the world's most thrilling structures. His first gig out of university was the roof of the Sydney Opera House – talk about in at the deep end. He helped fashion the Pompidou Centre and Louvre Pyramid in Paris, the Lloyd's building in London and the longest building in the world, the 1-mile (1.6km) long Kansai International Airport in Japan. This emerged from the Kobe earthquake without so much as a broken pane of glass, and today in 2001 was named 'Civil Engineering Monument of the Millennium'.

ARE YOU SURE THAT'S THE SAME DOLPHIN?

Since he was first spotted in Dingle harbour on this day in 1983, Fungie has become the most famous dolphin in the world. Nowhere else has a dolphin stayed for so long in the wild while interacting with humans. Even the attractions of passing female dolphins haven't been able to tear him away. It simply seems that Fungie's favourite thing in the world is pratting about in Dingle bay for the benefit of tourists. God bless him. Mind you, given that he's getting on a bit and that he attracts up to 200,000 tourists (with their wallets) every year, the town has now wisely immortalised Fungie with a bronze sculpture.

FECKIN' FANTASTIC

It's not just one of the funniest sitcoms ever, but an Irish institution. *Father Ted* was written by Irish writers Arthur Mathews and Graham Linehan, and the first of its 25 episodes transported delighted viewers to Craggy Island today in 1995. There, they joined the wild and wonderful world of Father Ted Crilly, Father Dougal McGuire, Father Jack Hackett and their housekeeper Mrs Doyle. It's one of those rare shows where you can be having the crappiest day ever, and if you just picture a character or think of a line, you find yourself laughing at life again.

WHISKEY IS GO-GO

It's official – people have been getting langered on whiskey in Ireland longer than anywhere else in the world. The Old Bushmills Distillery, Co. Antrim, founded in 1608, is the oldest licensed distillery on the planet. Of course, that's just when they 'fessed up to the excise man, we all know the mountain dew has been flowing as long as men have walked this land and had a thirst. And today in 2008, its importance was truly recognised when the Bushmills Distillery replaced Queen's University on Bank of Ireland notes.

A GOOD MAN TRIUMPHS

'The only thing necessary for evil to triumph is for good men to do nothing' is a powerful, beautiful thought, and it was expressed today in 1770 by Irishman Edmund Burke. This statesman, political theorist and philosopher wrote some of the most influential pamphlets of all time – his *Reflections on the French Revolution* was a landmark in international political theory that caused a sensation when published. Thomas Paine penned the *Rights of Man* in 1791 as a response to Burke's writings.

STORMIN' NORMAN

'If you're good enough, you're old enough' so the saying goes, and Norman Whiteside was both. The Belfast-born footballer made his professional debut today in 1982, aged just 16. He became the youngest player to score in an English League Cup and FA Cup final, and the youngest player to score a senior goal for Manchester United. In 1982 he broke Pelé's record as the youngest player in a World Cup, at 17 years and 41 days. Curiously, he heard he'd been offered terms by Manchester United while meeting US President Jimmy Carter on a school trip.

AHEAD OF THE GAME

There are some things it really, really doesn't pay to be first at. You might have read that the original victim of the guillotine was a French highwayman, Nicolas Pelletier, today in 1792. Not so – it was actually Murcod Ballagh, a rogue from Co. Wexford. He had his head sliced off way back in 1307, near Merton on the River Slaney. Still, at least it shows that Irish manufacturers of killing machines were centuries ahead of their French counterparts.

TO MONTO, PRONTO

Forget IT and finance, in the 19th century, Dublin was a world leader in a more earthy business field. For at that time Montgomery Street was the largest red-light district in Europe. At least 1,600 ladies of negotiable affection conducted their business, and the future King Edward VII lost his virginity there. This specialisation was immortalised in the song 'Take Me Up To Monto' by The Dubliners, recorded today in 1966.

THANK THE WOLVES

In the 16th century the Dublin and Wicklow mountains were overrun with wolves. Oliver Cromwell was so worried about this that he published a declaration in Kilkenny today, in 1652, that insisted locals continue to breed sufficient numbers of the mighty hounds that they used to hunt the beasts. Dublin's lupine population is less worrying nowadays, but those hunting dogs are still with us. The Irish Wolfhound is today a popular symbol of the country, and the world's tallest breed of dog.

IT NEARLY ADDS UP FOR LUDGATE

 Who knows what that quiet guy in the finance department is on the brink of becoming. Percy Ludgate was a Dublin accountant who today, in 1909, published a design for an analytical engine – one of the world's first computers. Ludgate did this independently in his spare time, without any knowledge of the work of earlier computer pioneer, Charles Babbage. His device was brilliant: fully programmable, it would have performed all arithmetical functions, using multiplication as its base mechanism, where Babbage's machine used addition. Alas it was never built, and the quiet Irish accountant missed his chance to become the Edwardian Steve Jobs.

KEARNEY DUCKS THE BULLETS

 Only in Ireland would both sides pause an armed insurrection so a man could feed his ducks. During the Easter Rising of April 1916, the rebels holed up on one side of St Stephen's Green and British soldiers on another, shooting at each other across the park square. But when colourful groundskeeper James Kearney heard the shots and a young rebel told him, 'Sir, the revolution has started!' Kearney gruffly replied, 'There'll be no bloody revolution on my green.' And for the duration of the fighting he walked out every day between the rifles to feed his rare birds. Both sides respectfully stopped shooting. Once the ducks had had their lunch, they got back on with killing each other again.

EURO HEROES

 Eurovision is ours. We've just got the thing licked. We've won it a record seven times, and today, in 1994, became the first and only country to bag it three years in a row. Paul Harrington and Charlie McGettigan scooped the honours on home turf (the Point Theatre, Dublin) with a song written by Brendan Graham, 'Rock 'n' Roll Kids'.

MAY

BELTANE GOES BIG

1 Today will see thousands of people take to mountains, forests and rural hideaways across Ireland, and the wider world, to celebrate Beltane. Once a solemn Celtic festival marking the return of summer, it's now mostly an excuse to get wrecked, get your kit off and prance about a hilltop with a bunch of other happy nutters.

REASONS TO BE CHEERFUL

Radiotherapy took an atomic leap forwards thanks to John Joly from Co. Offaly. He was first man to use radiation to treat cancerous tumours. Today in 1914 he published his pioneering 'Dublin method' of using a hollow needle for deep radiotherapy, a technique that later entered worldwide use. He was also the first person to successfully produce a colour photograph from a single plate. Hopefully it wasn't a picture of a tumour, but something nice, like a kitten.

A BELOW-PAR PERFORMANCE

Barry Fitzgerald was an Irish actor who made his name in Sean O'Casey plays and then Hollywood movies, such as *The Quiet Man*. He also achieved a feat unmatched in the history of the Academy Awards: he was nominated for both the Best Actor and the Best Supporting Actor awards for the same performance, as 'Father Fitzgibbon' in *Going My Way* (released today in 1944). Thankfully he won one of them (Best Supporting Actor), although he did later break the head off his Oscar statuette while enthusiastically practising his golf swing.

ANYTHING YOU CAN DO

The Yeats family was certainly a talented one: Jack was poet William's brother, but he wasn't about to live in his shadow. While William won the Nobel Prize, Jack did something even more remarkable: he became Ireland's first-ever Olympic medallist. The 1924 Olympic Games (which opened today) was the first time the Irish Free State had entered the competition. Yeats won a silver medal in the arts and culture segment of the Games for his painting *The Liffey Swim*.

IRISH DANCE STEPS UP

Riverdance was only ever supposed to be a titbit to fill a seven-minute gap between performances at the 1994 Eurovision Song Contest. But after it got a standing ovation, the music hit number one today, and stayed there for 18 weeks over the summer. The damn thing then mutated into a stage show, video, tour and arena-filling global brand. Like it or loathe it, it's how much of the world sees Irish music and dance.

THE RIDDLE OF THE MAN

As both a loyal supporter of the British Empire and an extreme Irish nationalist, it's fair to say that Robert Erskine Childers was a complex character. Politics aside, he was also a brilliant writer, whose masterpiece *The Riddle of the Sands* was published today in 1903. It was immediately wildly popular, has never gone out of print, and is considered to be the first spy novel. Winston Churchill said its realistic portrayal of an invasion led directly to Britain establishing a series of naval bases in case of war with Germany. Childers was executed in the civil war, but his son, Erskine Hamilton Childers, became the fourth President of Ireland.

UNSHAKEABLE CONFIDENCE

Sometimes it seemed he just couldn't miss – Ronan O'Gara was the rugby player with a laser-targeting system in his head and a cannon in his boot. He won his first international cap in 2000 and went on to be the highest points scorer not just for Munster and Ireland, but in the Heineken Cup and the whole Six Nations. Cheekily, he was also the player who didn't shake Queen Elizabeth II's hand today in 2009, when she congratulated Ireland on their first Grand Slam in 61 years.

FIRST CLASS TRAVEL

8 This was a train set worthy of admiration – it ferried stout around the Guinness brewery. From 1873, Samuel Geoghegan designed his own narrow-gauge steam locomotives and laid 8 miles (13km) of track in the St James's Gate premises. A unique spiral tunnel turned 2.5 revolutions under St James's Street, connecting the high and low parts of the brewery. Today in 1888, Geoghegan introduced ingenious convertor wagons that allowed the 1ft 10in- (37.4cm-) gauge locomotives to travel on the broad-gauge lines outside the brewery – so the beer could get to the pubs faster.

BLOOD BY NAME

Thomas Blood from Co. Clare spent much of his life hatching kidnap and murder plots, and today in 1671 he made the most famous attempt to steal the English crown jewels. He fooled the aged Master of the Jewel House at the Tower of London, Talbot Edwards, into thinking his nephew would marry Edwards' daughter. At the 'meeting' his gang assaulted Edwards and pinched the jewels. Blood was caught, but refused to answer to anyone but King Charles II. Blood must have had some blarney in him, because not only was he fully pardoned by Charles, but was also given land in Ireland and a pension worth £500 a year.

BRACKEN'S BLARNEY

Winston Churchill wasn't even going to stand as Prime Minister today in 1940 until Brendan Bracken from Templemore, Co. Tipperary persuaded him it might be a good idea. The son of a mason, Bracken blagged his way into English society and became a wealthy publisher and politician. He bought the *Financial Times* and turned it into the world's premier financial newspaper. As Minister for Information in the Second World War, he was George Orwell's boss: Bracken's nickname – 'BB' – and behaviour inspired the character of 'Big Brother' in his book *1984*.

SOMEONE LEFT THE
WHAT OUT IN THE RAIN?

There have been many hell-raising Irish actors, but Limerick-born Richard Harris was one of the greatest. When he wasn't getting pissed with Peter O'Toole and Richard Burton he was making terrific movies such as *The Guns of Navarone*, *Mutiny on the Bounty*, *The Wild Geese*, *Gladiator* and two Harry Potter films. Harris was also a talented rugby player, poet and singer – he famously released an unforgettable recording of 'MacArthur Park' today in 1968. To some it's a classic seven-minute psychedelic odyssey, to others it's a barking-mad rant. Either way, it's very, very Harris.

HEAVENLY HALL

Not many venues have had such an eclectic mix of performers tread their boards as Belfast's Ulster Hall. Since its opening night today in 1862, its walls have resounded to voices as varied as Mick Jagger, Debbie Harry, Ian Paisley, AC/DC and Charles Dickens. Its pipe organ is one of the finest of its type in the world, and the hall is also where Led Zeppelin first performed their legendary tune 'Stairway to Heaven'.

NOW COUGH

The next time your doctor listens to your chest for five seconds and fobs you off with some antibiotics, you can thank Arthur Leared from Wexford. For it was he who invented the 'binaural' stethoscope – the design with two earpieces. Leared first presented a model of this 'double' stethoscope at the Great Exhibition in London today in 1851. Originally made of gutta-percha, Leared's instrument was refined within a few years to pretty much the one that gives you shivers today.

BOYZONE'S BOY BAND BRILLIANCE

Who doesn't love Boyzone? Well, whatever you personally think of them, you can't deny that they've been an unbelievably successful Irish export. Officially, since their first release today in 1994, Boyzone have had 21 top 40 singles in the Irish charts, 19 singles in the UK charts and dozens more worldwide. This tally includes nine number ones, five number one albums and 25 million records sold worldwide to date. Unofficially, they have also probably had more pairs of knickers flung at them than any other group in history.

THE CHEESY TASTE OF SUCCESS

Crisps would be pretty boring if all they tasted of was potato. But that's all they did taste of until today in 1954: that's when Irishman Joe 'Spud' Murphy, boss of Tayto, cooked up the first-ever batch of flavoured crisps – Cheese & Onion. It was an immediate hit, and Murphy had bagged a winner. In 2009, Cheese & Onion finally eclipsed Ready Salted as the nation's number one flavour. Must be something to do with the credit crunch.

AND THE WINNER IS...CEDRIC

You probably haven't heard of Cedric Gibbons from Dublin, but every year you see his statue. He was a Hollywood art director whose production designs had a massive influence on movies. He also helped found the Academy of Motion Picture Arts and Sciences and designed the famous Oscar statuette, the first of which was awarded tonight in 1929. Cedric went on to win 11 of them himself. Gibbons also had a famous nephew – Billy Gibbons, guitarist and singer in ZZ Top.

FAME IS RELATIVE

Einstein was a one-off genius who plucked special relativity from the depths of his brain and changed science – er, actually no. His revelations were the pinnacle of many little steps and one big one made by George FitzGerald, a professor of physics at Trinity College, Dublin. Today in 1889, 20 years before relativity, FitzGerald answered a seemingly incomprehensible physics problem by suggesting that fast-moving objects shrink along their direction of travel. It seemed bonkers at the time, but now it's called the FitzGerald-Lorentz length contraction and it became an essential part of Einstein's theory.

DUNLOP CHANGES UP A GEAR

Moving to Ireland can have a powerful – even positive – effect on people. John Boyd Dunlop was a Scottish vet whose career rolled in a very different direction after moving to Ireland in 1867. Wheels in those days were made of solid iron, wood and rubber. Dunlop pitied the rough ride his son was getting on his tricycle and started to experiment. In 1888 he patented the first practical inflatable tyre. The following spring, the captain of the Belfast Cruisers Cycling Club bought a bicycle fitted with Dunlop's tyres and today, in 1889, he won all four cycling events at the Queen's College Sports in Belfast.

IF IT DOESN'T CLEAR UP
IN A WEEK, TRY GIN

19 It's often said that soda water was invented by Robert Percival, Professor of Chemistry at Trinity College, Dublin on this day in 1800. To be honest, this isn't strictly true: soda water had already been produced by Thomas Henry in England in the 1770s. Percival's genius lay in pioneering its 'medicinal' use – which probably means he was the first person to add whiskey.

THE IDEA WAS MINE

20 Mining was a hideously dangerous job in the early 19th century. The presence of flammable gases in the pit meant that the only source of light, your lamp, could very well blow you to pieces. Bangor physician William Clanny came up with the very first safety lamp, which used water to cut out the flammable gases. His paper was read to the Royal Society today in 1813, and within a few years he had used a working model at a pit in Sunderland. Englishman Humphry Davy saw this and later invented his own famous version of the mining lamp – while acknowledging that Clanny had got there before him.

BRAVERY OF THE HIGHEST ORDER

One of the best, and bravest, mountaineers of his generation was Gerard McDonnell. In 2008 he became the first Irish person to summit K2, but on the way down he perished with ten others in the worst-ever accident on that mountain. The surviving members of McDonnell's team said he refused point blank to descend until he'd helped the injured. We can also be proud of his achievement today in 2003 – Ger became the highest ball-sports player in world history when he pucked a sliotar off the South Col of Mount Everest on his way to the summit. Apparently it was in an effort to banish the demons of Limerick hurling...

THE HIGHEST OF HONOURS

He was the beautiful boy with a beautiful game, one of the most naturally talented footballers ever to pull on a pair of boots. Belfast-born George Best won the English league title, the European Cup, and European Player of the Year award at the age of 22. Alas, the high life took its toll – 'I spent a lot of money on booze, birds and fast cars. The rest I just squandered.' Today in 2006, on what would have been Best's 60th birthday, Belfast City Airport was renamed in his honour, the only one in the world named after a footballer.

A GOOD DAY FOR DUCKS

If you enjoy pottering along a leafy waterway in a boat with the sun on your back and a drink in your hand (and who doesn't?), then today's a day worth mooring up on. For it was at a ceremony today in 1994 at Corraguil Lock, Teemore, Co. Fermanagh that the Shannon–Erne Waterway was officially opened. This created Europe's longest inland navigable waterway (249 miles/400km long), a haven for rare wetland birds and the greatest collection of riverside boozers you're ever likely to drift past.

CLEARED FOR TAKE OFF

In the 1920s the world had gone aviation crazy, and Sophie Pierce-Evans from Limerick was one of the most famous women on the planet. She was the first woman in the British Isles with a pilot's licence and boy, did she put it to good use: she set a world altitude record, became the first woman to make a parachute jump and the first to loop the loop. Today in 1928 she was the first person to fly solo from Cape Town to London. She even held the world high jump record.

MACNEILL KEEPS THE WORLD MOVING

When it came to transport, Sir John Benjamin Macneill was a mover and a shaker. The civil engineer from Co. Louth was a vital help to Thomas Telford in many of his revolutionary projects, including the massive London–Holyhead road. Macneill pioneered several innovative railway projects, including the Dublin and Drogheda Railway (opened today in 1844). Most of Ireland's modern railway network follows his routes, and he designed the famously bonkers Macneill's Egyptian Arch in Newry, on the border between Co. Armagh and Co. Down. Macneill was also a noted teacher of civil engineering – his pupils included Sir Joseph Bazalgette, the man who installed London's sewage system.

THE CREATION THAT WOULD NOT DIE

Not many authors are influential enough to create not just a character or a story, but an actual legend. Dublin-born Bram Stoker is one of those rare few. Vampire myths are ancient, but it was Stoker's novel *Dracula* (published today in 1897) that set the template for the quintessential blood-sucker. The aristocratic background, the castle, the shape-shifting, the accent, the outfit, the predilection for puncturing pretty young ladies – Stoker brought them all together and created the Count. *Twilight* fans have him to thank for making vampires suave and sexy...

PFIZER RISER

There's a town in Ireland that has made more men proud than any other place on the planet – Ringaskiddy, Co. Cork. The Pfizer pharmaceutical company erected an impressive plant there, and since this day in 1998, it has satisfied the world's demand for Viagra. Millions of men (and a similar number of women) are grateful, if a little tired right now. Oh, and it can't be a coincidence that the plant is just 20 miles (32km) from the Blarney Stone...

SHORTHAND FOR SUCCESS

28 You might not have heard of John Robert Gregg from Monaghan, but he made hundreds of thousands of newspaper headlines. He published a fast and efficient form of stenography today in 1888, called Gregg shorthand. It took the US by storm, with journalists and court reporters favouring it. While dictation machines and smartphones put the writing on the wall for shorthand, Gregg's notation is still popular.

NO, I DON'T WANT A FRIGGIN' SCRATCHCARD

Say what you like about the experience of flying Ryanair (and most of us could probably think of a few choice things off the top of our heads) it is certainly a proud Irish success story. Since it took off in 1984 with one plane, and through public flotation on this day 12 years later, it has become one of Europe's biggest airlines, with 8,500 members of staff and 1,200 pilots. It brings more people to Ireland than any other carrier – who cares if they're grumpy as all hell when they get here!

MAY

SAY CH-CH-CH-CH-CH-CH-CH-CHEESE!

Can I take a quick picture, love? Lucien Bull from Dublin moved to Paris in order to work as an assistant for Étienne-Jules Marey, a cinematography pioneer. Bull devised a high-speed version of Marey's camera, which was the first in the world able to photograph insects in flight and projectiles such as a bullet piercing a soap bubble. In 1904, Bull achieved 1,200 images per second. By today in 1924, he'd managed 100,000 images per second and by 1952, one million images per second – by far the fastest camera the world had seen at that time.

THIS PARTY'S STARTING A BIT LATE, ISN'T IT?

You can imagine the meeting in 1985 – 'I know, let's give Dublin a boost by celebrating its 1,000th birthday!' 'Magic idea!' The only problem was that the city was founded in AD 841 by the Vikings, and since time travel wasn't available to the local authorities, 1988 was plucked out of fresh air. To be fair, lots of good things were achieved that year – the Anna Livia monument ('the floozie in the Jacuzzi'), a commemorative milk bottle and a new 50p piece (minted today). And it's worth noting that Dublin is in fact the oldest Norse capital in the world – the next contender, Reykjavik, wasn't established for another 30 years.

JUNE

MARTIN'S MAGIC

Not many brilliant footballers also make it as brilliant managers – Martin O'Neill is one of those few. As a player he was capped 64 times for Northern Ireland and captained the side that reached the quarter-finals of the 1982 World Cup. He also won the 1980 European Cup with Nottingham Forest. As a manager, many of his clubs consider him their most successful gaffer ever – Wycombe Wanderers, Norwich City and Leicester City, for example. He was appointed Celtic boss today in 2000, and in his first season guided them to the treble.

WHAT DID YOU DO IN THE HOLIDAYS?

Like any serious students on a field trip, JM Dickenson and Brian Varley goofed off today in 1952 and began to explore some cliffs near Lisdoonvarna, Co. Clare. Keen cavers, they saw a small stream disappearing into a huge limestone cliff. They cleared away some rocks and wriggled along a tiny passage for ¼ mile (400m), as you do, until they came into a wider space. Hoping to have discovered a new cave, they turned their torches upward and discovered, hanging from the roof, the longest stalactite in the northern hemisphere. The awesome Great Stalactite in the Doolin Cave measures 24ft (7.3m) and now draws rock fans from around the world.

(NOT) ON THE MONEY

It's no wonder the economy is in such a state, considering our relationship with cash. The Republic has had five currencies in the last 100 years – sterling until 1928, the Saorstát pound (Free State pound) for ten years from 1928, the Irish pound after that, then the decimalised pound in 1971, and the Euro from 1999. In Northern Ireland it's worse: banknotes have been issued since today in 1929, and are legal currency, but technically not legal tender anywhere, including Northern Ireland itself. They are of course accepted, but really only have the same standing as cheques.

DEATH PENALTY

What sports fan doesn't love the drama of a penalty shootout? Well, for that we can be proud of William McCrum from Co. Armagh. This merchant's son and keen goalkeeper had more money than skill – his team Milford once finished bottom of the league with zero points from 14 games, scoring ten goals and conceding 62. The game was then blighted with violent, sometimes deadly, tackles on forwards through on goal. So McCrum proposed the idea of the penalty kick, submitting it today in 1890 to the International Football Association Board. 'Gentlemen' players were outraged at first at this 'death penalty', but it was written into the rulebook the next year.

ONE COOL DUDE

Given the less-than-tropical state of our weather, it's fitting that an Irishman invented the temperature scale based on Absolute Zero. William Thomson, 1st Baron Kelvin, was the Belfast-born physicist who created the Kelvin scale, which starts at -273.15°C (-459.67°F), today in 1848. Appropriately, the Kelvinator brand of fridges is named after him.

JUNE

HAMMER TIME

The hammer throw is an ancient sport, but it was only really launched into the modern athletic world thanks to John Flanagan from Kilbreedy, Co. Limerick. Flanagan crushed opponents, often throwing 170ft (51.8m) when the second place athlete only managed 120ft (36.6m). This domination won him three Olympic gold medals in a row in 1900, 1904, and 1908. The improvements he made are remarkable for any sport – he broke the world record for the 15th time today in 1909 and over a 13-year career he added more than 37ft (11.3m) to the mark.

YER MAN IS A WINNER

There haven't been many motorbike champions more beloved than Joey Dunlop from Ballymoney, Co. Antrim. His achievements include three hat-tricks at the Isle of Man TT meeting (1985, 1988 and 2000), and today in 2000 he won a record 26th TT in 25 years of competing. During his career he won the Ulster Grand Prix 24 times, and in 1986 he won a fifth consecutive TT Formula One world title. Outside of the racing season, Joey made endless trips to deliver food and clothing to Romanian orphans – thankfully in a van, though, not on his bike.

FISTS AND FLAMBÉES

Winning fights is one thing, winning hearts is another. Barry McGuigan was brilliant at both. Born in the border town of Clones, Co. Monaghan, he boxed for Northern Ireland in the 1978 Commonwealth Games and for Ireland at the 1980 Moscow Olympics. His non-sectarian approach to sport won him fans from all sides, and today in 1985 he became World Featherweight Champion in front of 26,000 ecstatic fans in London. He was later named BBC Sports Personality of the Year, the first ever recipient not born in the UK. He also won TV show *Hell's Kitchen*, showing how tough he really is...

ST COLUMBA©

Today we (and particularly publishers) celebrate the feast of St Colmcille (or Columba), the 6th-century Irish abbot. He earns a fair bit of respect for taking Christianity to the barbarian Picts and defying the Loch Ness Monster, but also notable was his refusal to hand over a copy of St Finnian's psalms that he had made in secret. King Diarmuid famously ruled on this matter: 'To every cow its calf and to every book its copy.' This is regarded as the world's first copyright judgement, and is still a fundamental right in Irish Law.

JUNE

LAYTOWN BEACH RACE

The last time 11,000 people were on an Irish beach was when the natives were trying to repel the Vikings. But these days it's for a meet at Laytown, Co. Meath – the only official horse race in Europe run on a beach. The first recorded meeting was today in 1868, when beach races were run with the Boyne Regatta. The rowing was at high tide, the racing at low. Since then the gallop down the 3 mile (4.8km) golden strand has become one of the world's unique sporting events. Jockeys have to be careful though – you do not know pain until you've had sand in your jodhpurs.

WIND-POWERED WORLD-BEATERS

When Francis Chichester was looking for a world-beating boat in which to cross the Atlantic, he turned to expert shipbuilders in Arklow, Co. Wicklow. Today in 1960, his Irish-built *Gipsy Moth III* set off for New York and arrived after 40 days at sea, slashing 16 days off the previous fastest time. There must be something in the wind around Arklow's shores, because it's also the site of the world's first offshore wind turbines over 3 megawatts in size.

GET THE GIFT OF THE GAB/HERPES

12 Ever since Cormac MacCarthy, the builder of Blarney Castle, was granted the eloquence to win a lawsuit by the goddess Clíodhna, the Blarney Stone has conferred the gift of the gab on all who kiss it. Mind you, this isn't easy to do. You have to climb to the top of the castle then dangle backwards over the edge of the parapet to reach the thing. Still it draws the punters (400,000 of them a year), which is probably why today in 2009 it was voted the most unhygienic tourist attraction in the world.

A-LIVE A-LIVE O!

Ah, sweet Molly Malone, that famous Dublin girl – beautiful, voice like an angel, destined to die young. Except she never really existed and the song was written by a Scotsman. Still, the Irish are nothing if not creative, and we won't let the mere truth get in the way of a good story, particularly if it helps sell a T-shirt. So, today in 1988 was declared the first annual 'Molly Malone Day', and a statue of a rather busty Molly and her barrow was erected. She is affectionately known to the locals as 'The Tart With The Cart'.

STILL THE BEST

Now here's an Irish invention we can raise a proud toast to. Dublin-born Aeneas Coffey's early career wasn't very impressive – the man was a high-flier in the excise service, for goodness' sake. But thankfully he gave up taxing booze to perfect making the stuff. His finest creative moment came today in 1830, when he patented the single column still, which made spirit smoother. Soon nearly every liquor producer in Europe and the Americas had a Coffey still. Rum, gin, vodka, blended Scotch, and blended Irish whiskey all became more palatable, and output went through the roof.

NOW WASH YOUR BLOODY HANDS!

It's not every day that someone goes down in history for being a filthy mare. But today in 1907, Mary Mallon from Cookstown, Co. Tyrone, did just that. She was identified as the cause of several deadly typhoid outbreaks in New York – the first healthy typhoid carrier known to medical science. After emigrating to the US, 'Typhoid Mary' worked as a cook, possibly the single worst job she could have taken. She never washed her hands before cooking, refused to believe she was a carrier and kept running away from the authorities and changing her name. Eventually she was forcibly kept in quarantine for the last 30 years of her life.

BLOOMSDAY

James Joyce said he wanted to capture the sights, sounds and characters of a day in the Irish capital so that if it were wiped from the map it could be recreated. You can see how he managed this in his masterpiece *Ulysses*, the action of which all takes place on this single day in 1904. Well, if you are able to make head or tail of the thing. Today the novel's hero, Leopold Bloom, is remembered by Joyce fans that flock to the city and who, rather than doing any reading, mostly celebrate the day by visiting the various bars mentioned in the text.

EXPLORING A NEW TYPE OF ART

Paul Kane from Mallow, Co. Cork, was a self-taught painter who today, in 1845, started a series of remarkable wanderings in the wilds of Canada. Venturing where few Europeans had ever been before, Kane travelled thousands of miles in brutal conditions to sketch the native people and record their lives. This feat, unequalled by any other artist ever, produced an utterly unique ethnological document as well as some beautiful pictures.

WELLINGTON WINS THE DAY

When the Duke of Wellington's forces defeated Napoleon at the Battle of Waterloo today in 1815, it was a proud day for Irishmen everywhere. After all, Arthur Wellesley was born in what is now Dublin's Merrion Hotel, spent much of his childhood in Ireland and got his first job here. Not that the snooty duke was proud of it. He is reputed to have said of his origins: 'Being born in a stable does not make one a horse.' But as he also invented the welly boot, we can forgive him.

RORY ROARS TO THE TOP

There's winning, and then there's winning Rory McIlroy-style. When the golfer from Holywood, Co. Down won the 2011 US Open today, in 2011, his score of 268 (16 under par), was eight shots clear of everyone else, and was a new US Open record that sliced (actually it was more of a fade) an amazing four shots off the previous best held by Jack Nicklaus and Tiger Woods. He was just 22 years old. The next year, for his second major championship victory, he won the PGA Championship by a record eight strokes. Mind you, it was always going to happen – McIlroy hit a 40-yard (36.6m) drive at the age of two.

THE ROMANS ROAM ON

We can be proud of our Celtic ancestors for making us one of the very, very few European countries not conquered by Rome. When the Roman general Agricola became governor of Britain (arriving today in AD 77), he apparently fancied his chances of conquering Ireland. He believed he could take and hold the country with one legion plus auxiliaries. He had a wee shot at it too, crossing over for a short time in AD 82. But he didn't stay long and he didn't do any conquering. Chances are he took one look at the food on offer and left us to it.

A VERY SPECIAL CEREMONY

The world had never seen anything like it. Today in 2003 saw the triumphant opening of the Special Olympics in Dublin, with the event being held for the first time ever outside the US. During ten days of contests, 7,000 athletes would participate in 21 sports and thousands more volunteers gave their time and talents. It was the 2003 games that dramatically changed how wider society viewed the potential of people with physical and intellectual disabilities. Dublin was also the first venue to broadcast the opening and closing ceremonies live.

LINEN IT UP

When the American Civil War began in 1861 it was the start of four years of hard times for the country's citizens. It also caused disaster in England's cotton mills. An unexpected benefit was that Irish linen took up much of the slack. Even by the end of the war, today in 1865, the linen trade was unstoppable, with Belfast – nicknamed 'Linenopolis' – the largest linen-producing area in the world. This boom wouldn't begin to fray around the edges for decades.

RING OF LOVE

It fits neatly in the hand, warms the heart and is a well-known Irish way of showing someone that you love them – no, not a shot of Jameson's, but a Claddagh ring. The symbolic hands-holding-a-heart design had long been worn in the Galway area, but came to wider attention today in 1903 with the publication of an article by jeweller William Dillon. It soon became known as a loving symbol and is now popular worldwide, particularly in America.

EIGHT-LEGGED IRISH INSPIRATION

Robert the Bruce is one of Scotland's greatest heroes, famous for defeating the English at the Battle of Bannockburn (today in 1314), and forging an independent nation. But what's not so well-known is that after defeat at the Battle of Perth in 1306, he holed up in a cave on Rathlin Island, Co. Antrim. And it was here that he watched a spider patiently trying again and again to spin a web across an impossible gap until it eventually succeeded. Inspired, Bruce returned from exile and defeated his enemies. So the famous Scot owes his legendary victory to an Irish spider!

JUNE

WE'VE HADDOCK-NOUGH OF THIS NONSENSE

 To most people in Dublin he was plain old John from the chip shop. But the polite old gent was really one of the world's great revolutionaries. His real name was Ivan Beshoff and he was part of the mutiny on the battleship *Potemkin* (today in 1905), which helped spawn the Bolshevik Revolution and inspired one of the greatest films ever made (*Battleship Potemkin*). Beshoff and crew rebelled against the cruel treatment by officers, and he later settled in Ireland and founded a famously tasty chain of chippers.

BRENDAN THE BOLD

 Did an Irish monk discover America 1,000 years before Columbus? Yes, so the supporters of 6th-century religious rover St Brendan say. Brendan wrote a famous text about his seven-year voyage, and most people thought it was just one of those, you know, allegory things. But then navigation expert Tim Severin built a replica of Brendan's currach using traditional tools and materials, and sailed it 4,474 miles (7,200km) from Ireland to Newfoundland, landing safely today in 1977.

METAL DETECTED

When a mining company dug a hole near Navan, Co. Meath in 1969, they saw nothing and walked away. When a different company tried again four years later, they had a bit more Irish luck, and struck gold – well, zinc. The largest deposit in Europe, in fact. First opened today in 1977, the Tara mine is now one of the largest of its type in the world, hauling 200,000 tons of zinc and lead from ²/₃ mile (1km) below the surface every year.

YOU'RE NO MATE OF MINE

You know you're getting good when your coach refuses to play against you. Alexander McDonnell from Belfast became so brilliant at chess that his teacher, previously the greatest player in Britain, decided to protect his reputation and declined to play. But McDonnell really went down in history today in 1834, when he began a legendary series of matches against French chess genius La Bourdonnais. Considered the first chess championship, McDonnell won the second match, making him briefly World Champion. These matches contained such innovative moves that they are considered to be the birth of modern chess.

WHEELY TALENTED

Isabel Woods of Lisburn, Co. Antrim/Co. Down, was a cycling prodigy who did more than anyone else in the world to raise the profile of women's cycling. She notched up eight world records in the 1950s, one of which stood as one of the longest records in cycling, and indeed in any sport. Her time for the Ladies 'End-to-End' Irish cycling record, from Mizen Head in Co. Cork to Fair Head, Co. Antrim, which she set today in 1955, stood until July 2007 – 52 years.

PEAK PERFORMANCE

You might think it's hard enough climbing Mount Everest, even more so when you go snowblind. But today, in 2007, Irishman Ian McKeever completed an ascent of that mountain, plus the six other highest peaks on each continent, in just 156 days. This smashed the world record for a 'Seven Summits' speed ascent by a full month. He also helped hundreds of Irish teenagers climb Mount Kilimanjaro, which might have been the trickier challenge.

JULY

A NATION WITH PLUCK

There's no doubt we're a musical country – Ireland is the only nation in the world to have a musical instrument as its symbol. It's been our heraldic mark at least since Henry VIII was proclaimed king today in 1542, but it probably goes back much further. The current 1920s design is based on the Brian Boru harp at Trinity College, Dublin, although the design did have to be flipped to face left to avoid any shenanigans regarding the trademark of a certain brand of stout.

GREEN MACHINES

'British Racing Green' isn't anything of the sort – it's 'Irish Green'. Today in 1903 saw the first ever international motor race in Ireland, the Gordon Bennett cup. It was held here because, at the time, racing on public roads was illegal in Britain. It wasn't 100 per cent allowed in Ireland either – local laws covering the Kildare course had to be 'adjusted': the Bishop of Kildare and Leighlin declared himself in favour, and the 'Light Locomotives (Ireland) Bill' was passed today in 1903 to make the thing fully legal. As a compliment to Ireland the British team raced in shamrock green – only later did this become known as British racing green.

THEY CERTAINLY MADE A SPLASH

When record (and headline) chasers Richard Branson and Per Lindstrand tried to balloon across the Atlantic for the first time, the good old Irish weather decided to remind them to keep their feet on the ground. Their balloon was the largest ever made – 21 storeys tall, it reached 115 mph (185km/h) at 30,000ft (9,146m). They made it across the ocean from Maine, but as they approached Rathlin Island, Co. Antrim, today in 1987, a squall tore into the balloon (and their pride) and the pair had to jump into the sea to save their lives.

JACKIE, ARE YOU SURE THAT'S HOW YOU SPELL IT?

It's one of the most significant meaningful documents in political history, and by Jesus they only went and trusted the printing of it to an Irishman. John Dunlap from Strabane, Co. Tyrone had won a lucrative contract printing the minutes and other materials of the Continental Congress. Then, on 2 July 1776, the Congress voted to secede from Britain – and two days later, Dunlap found himself printing 200 broadside copies of the *United States Declaration of Independence*, the document that would found a nation.

LATE AND GREAT

It was meant to be just an eight-week summer filler, but from its first broadcast tonight in 1962, Gay Byrne turned *The Late Late Show* into something historic. It's not just that he helmed it for 37 years, making it the world's longest-running chat show; 'Uncle Gaybo' broached taboo subjects, introduced fresh bands and put heads of state in living rooms across the land, making him a real power in Ireland's social change since the 1960s. No wonder he topped Presidential polls in 2011, despite not actually running. While working in Britain he even became the first person to introduce The Beatles on screen.

RADIO RATHLIN

To be fair, Guglielmo Marconi doesn't sound all that Irish, but he still goes down in this island's proud history. With his equipment, two of his employees made the world's first commercial wireless telegraph transmission between Ballycastle, Co. Antrim, and the East Lighthouse on Rathlin Island, today in 1898. The first successful transmission was just the single letter 'V' – not the most interesting of messages, but it was enough to prove the system worked.

TOP OF THE COPS

Modern police forces owe their existence and organisation to a man from Co. Antrim, Sir Charles Rowan. He was a soldier in the Napoleonic Wars before being selected by Sir Robert Peel as the first Commissioner of the Metropolitan Police, a role he took up today in 1829. Rowan was responsible for the organisation of the new force and in 12 weeks he managed to recruit, train, organise, equip and deploy a force of nearly 1,000 men. He designed the blue uniforms, and bought and furnished station houses. Even the idea of the policeman's 'beat' came from Rowan's military experience.

AN INDEPENDENT SPEAKER

And as if the events of four days ago weren't enough to place on a nation's shoulders, today the Yanks only entrusted Charles Thomson from Maghera, Co. Londonderry to read the thing to the people of the new republic. Thomson stood on the steps of the Philadelphia Statehouse, Pennsylvania a little after noon, and read the Declaration of Independence to a startled, and by all accounts slightly terrified, American populace. He also designed the Great Seal of the United States.

YOUR ROOM HAS AN EN SUITE SHOWER (OF PLASTER)

Only in Ireland would locals be proud about an establishment's claim to fame as 'The most bombed hotel in the world'. But that's just what the Europa in Belfast (opened today in 1971) is known for. To be fair, it has been bombed 28 times, so the fact that the poor building is still even standing is worthy of commemoration.

ROCHE AND ROLL

Only two men in history have won cycling's Triple Crown: the Giro d'Italia, World Road Race Championship and Tour de France. One of them is Stephen Roche from Dublin, in 1987. When Roche won the Tour's time trial today in 1987, everyone knew his remarkable feat was possible. But he famously nearly killed himself on Stage 21, collapsing over the line and being bundled into an ambulance. A doctor gave him oxygen and asked if Roche was okay. He replied, 'Oui, mais pas de femmes ce soir.' (Yes, but no women tonight.)

THIS MUSEUM IS A REVELATION

The Chester Beatty Library within Dublin Castle is one of the world's great collections of ancient religious manuscripts, and was named the European Museum of the Year today in 2002. 'Eclectic' doesn't begin to describe the collection: delicate Egyptian papyri, beautiful illuminated Korans and Hindu and Buddhist manuscripts, as well as the earliest known copies of the Book of Revelation, from AD 250, and of the Gospel of St John. A group of Amish visitors once broke into song when they saw the ancient pages, because the pieces of manuscript were the closest they had ever come to the original Scriptures.

GIRL POWER

They've been messing about in boats at the Royal Cork Yacht Club longer then anywhere else – founded in 1720, it's the world's oldest yacht club. The club was also the venue for the world's first motor boat race, the Harmsworth Cup. The inaugural race was run today in 1903, and won by an icon of female independence, Dorothy Levitt. In doing so she set the world's first Water Speed Record of 19.3mph (31.1km/h).

TECHNICALLY THE BEST

Opened today in 1975, Midleton in Co. Cork is one of the most modern distilleries in existence, with state-of-the-art fibre-optic communications that tell staff when the booze is ready. It produces the world's favourite Irish whiskey, Jameson, and the old, retired section of the distillery is a historic alcoholic marvel as well. Now a booze museum, it boasts the world's largest pot still – a colossal copper vessel with a capacity of 30,796 gallons (140,000l). That's a lot of hangovers.

LIKE SON, LIKE FATHER

14 William Wilde from Co. Roscommon was a forward-thinking eye and ear surgeon who pioneered the use of the drug atropine. He also helped the Irish census collect medical data that no other country in the world had at the time. With a very successful practice, he felt he should make some provision for the free treatment of the city's poor population and today, in 1844, he founded St Mark's Ophthalmic Hospital, built entirely at his own expense. But perhaps his greatest achievement was having an even more famous son, Oscar.

POLLUTION SOLUTION

15 Loafing in the garden of our holiday cottage in Adrigole, Co. Cork, on a hot summer's day, most of us would be musing on whether there were any beers in the fridge. Scientist James Lovelock, however, was wondering (today in 1968) whether the smog above the village was industrial pollution from Europe. He whipped out an electron capture detector of his own devising (as you do) and found the air was full of CFCs. These were doing heinous things to the ozone layer and were eventually banned. Adrigole was the first in a global network of atmospheric monitoring stations and the home of a new environmental movement.

HOBAN'S HOUSE

1600 Pennsylvania Avenue is one of the most famous buildings in the world – the White House. But in 1792, the residence of the US President was not the grand and imposing residence we see today: George Washington lived in cramped brick-built quarters in Philadelphia. So he held an architectural competition, which today was won by James Hoban from Kilkenny. Cheeky young Hoban pinched much of his elegant design from Leinster House in Dublin.

COYNE'S CARTOON CAPERS

Punch magazine was a British institution for decades, but its original creator was Joseph Stirling Coyne from Birr, Co. Offaly. One of the best-loved humourists of his day, Coyne wrote over 60 farces for the London stage. He led the meeting of creative gentlemen who dreamed up *Punch* in June 1841, and the first issue was published today. It was *Punch* that coined the word 'cartoon' in its modern sense as a humorous illustration.

DROP DEAD

Hanging just had no finesse before Samuel Haughton. The rope length rarely varied, so light victims dangled till they strangled, while fat ones were decapitated. Happily, however, the Carlow-born doctor applied scientific method to the process. He calculated a sliding scale of rope length to victim weight, designed to kill by cleanly breaking the neck. Haughton published his 'On hanging considered from a Mechanical and Physiological point of view' today, in 1866, and this 'Standard Drop' soon became the preferred method of humane execution the world over.

THE ROAD LESS TRAVELLED

Being selected to compete for your country aged just 18 is cool enough, but welterweight boxer Francis Barrett from Galway went a few steps further than that. He was selected to join the Irish Olympic team for the 1996 Atlanta Games, becoming its youngest member. He also carried the Irish flag during the opening ceremony, which took place today, and in so doing became the first member of the traveller community ever to carry a national flag at the Olympics.

DEAD KEEN TO LEARN

20 William Burke and William Hare were a pair of lowlife scumbags from Ulster who murdered 16 people in Edinburgh in the 1820s. Hardly types to be proud of, you might think. But hang on there – Burke and Hare had sold the cadavers to the local medical school, as it was desperately short of them. And the discovery of their crimes directly led to the passing of the Anatomy Act today in 1832, which gave students legal access to corpses and enabled medical science to leap forward. Forward-thinking boys indeed…

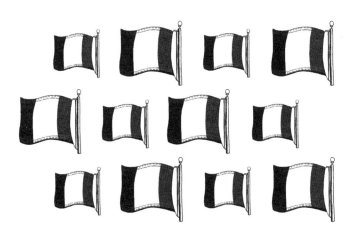

MARTIN WAS BARKING MAD

 The world's first piece of animal welfare legislation was known as Martin's Act, and it passed today, in 1822. It was proposed by Richard Martin from Galway, an MP and passionate activist who opposed bear baiting, dog fighting and other cruelty, and co-founded the RSPCA. Curiously, although kind to animals, Martin fought over 100 duels with humans. Many of these were over their mistreatment of animals. When Martin sued his wife's lover for £10,000 he gave the money to the poor by throwing it out the windows of his coach on the journey back to Galway.

'NOW DON'T BUGGER THIS ONE UP, BOYS'

 As building projects go, the Shannon Scheme was a monster – rivers were diverted, bridges built and a railway laid, all before the power station itself was constructed. The cost was £5.5 million, an astronomical amount considering that the new Irish state's entire budget was £25 million. But the boys did good – when inaugurated today in 1929 it was the largest source of hydroelectric power in the world, generating enough electricity for the whole country, and engineers came from far and wide to look and learn.

A SMASHING RESULT FOR IRELAND

 A historic Irish performance at the Wimbledon tennis championships was completed today in 1890, when Joshua Pim from Wicklow and Frank Stoker from Dublin won the men's doubles. Willoughby Hamilton from Kildare had already won the men's singles and Lena Rice from Co. Tipperary the ladies' competition. Furthermore, Rice became the first person in tennis history to use a smash shot in her final.

TOP GUN

 James Bond's Aston Martin wouldn't have dealt with bad guys in quite such an uplifting way if it wasn't for engineer James Martin from Crossgar, Co. Down. The co-founder of the Martin-Baker aircraft company made aviation history today in 1946, when he successfully tested the first modern ejection seat. Although ejection seats are intended to be used when a plane is flying, a few pilots have successfully ejected from under the sea, after being forced to ditch in water. Which is more Bond-like than Bond himself.

HARING INTO HISTORY

25 Mick the Miller from Killeigh, Co. Offaly, was one of the best performers in his field that the world has ever seen. And that wasn't actually milling, but running really fast after a make-believe rabbit – for our Mick was a greyhound. He set a world record in his first English Derby today in 1929, and went on to win 51 of the 68 races he entered, including an incredible 19 victories in a row.

THE WORD ON THE STREETS

Writers in some cities are remote figures stuck in dusty libraries, but in Dublin they have long been valued as part of the everyday landscape – well, at least good customers in the pubs. And today in 2010, this was recognised when Dublin became only the fourth place in the world to be awarded UNESCO City of Literature status. Four Nobel prizes have been won by writers associated with Dublin (Shaw, Yeats, Beckett, Heaney), more than most entire countries can manage, and Joyce would surely have got one too if he hadn't died a bit too early.

STYLE, WITH A CAPITAL SYBIL

Sybil Connolly turned Irish cheek into international chic: the fashion designer was inspired by traditional fabrics, with Donegal tweeds, Carrickmacross lace and Irish linen all making star appearances in her elegant collections. She invented a unique, uncrushable linen fabric by backing handkerchief linen with taffeta. When Jackie Kennedy visited Dublin today, in 1967, she snapped up a gown in this fabric. She then wore it in the famous portrait by Aaron Schickler that hangs in the White House.

POETS NEED PAIN

When the great Irish poet WB Yeats met the feisty revolutionary Maud Gonne it changed his life – he had found his muse. But it was a painful relationship for him: he proposed to her, and was rejected, five times (his first humiliation was today, in 1891). It was, however, also fruitful – Gonne once astutely told him, 'You would not be happy with me ... The world should thank me for not marrying you ... You make beautiful poetry out of what you call your unhappiness and you are happy in that.' She inspired at least 80 poems, including many of his most beautiful.

ARMAGEDDON OUT OF HERE

When he first proposed the existence of a disc of icy bodies beyond the orbit of Neptune today in 1943, nobody took Kenneth Edgeworth seriously. But observations later confirmed the existence of this reservoir of giant frozen rocks, and it's now known as the Edgeworth-Kuiper belt in honour of the Co. Westmeath astronomer. This might sound a bit academic, but it does help explain where comets come from. And so could presumably help us spot one that might be about to smash into us. Which certainly IS worth taking seriously.

HE'S GOT MORE TALENT IN HIS BIG TOE...

30 Premature babies the world over got a better chance at life thanks to Robert Collis, a doctor at Dublin's Rotunda Hospital. He invented a simple but affordable incubator for premature infants, and pioneered a technique for them via a nasal tube rather than a spoon. He also helped found Cerebral Palsy Ireland, and encouraged the artistic talents of one his early patients, editing the 21-year-old's autobiographical account of his daily struggle with life. Collis used his connections to help get the manuscript published, today in 1954 – and so *My Left Foot* by Christy Brown was brought to an amazed world.

THE WINNER BY A LENGTH

31 With a full week of racing, Galway Races is famous for being the longest meet in Ireland or Britain, and one of the biggest events in the world. Even more impressively, the pub underneath the Corrib Stand, which entertained race-goers for the first time today in 1955, was for many years the longest bar in the world. Alas, it was replaced in 1999, to the sight of long faces all round.

AUGUST

LUGHNACY

No, he wasn't the god of toilets. In fact, Lugh was a heroic sun god and a master of pretty much anything he turned his hand to. He was celebrated today with Lughnasadh, a festival of feasting, matchmaking and athletics. This celebration became the prototype for the harvest festival now held around the world. Today many people mark Lughnasadh by climbing a hill, which is nice, but if they were doing things properly they would eat some bilberries and sacrifice a bull when they got to the top.

AUGUST

POWER TO THE PEOPLE

Over 90 per cent of all electricity in the US today is produced by steam turbines, which were invented by Sir Charles Parsons, son of the Earl of Rosse, in 1884. Parson's first turbine produced 7.5kW, but could be easily scaled up, and the age of cheap and plentiful electricity had arrived. Parsons realised it could revolutionise transport, and today in 1894 he launched *Turbinia*, easily the fastest vessel on the world's oceans. He took her unannounced to that year's review of the British fleet, and in a brilliant publicity stunt zoomed in and out of the best ships of the Royal Navy, leaving them flailing in his wake. Large orders followed.

WAITING FOR GOOD REVIEWS

Literary master Samuel Beckett joined the all-time greats today in 1955, when his play *Waiting for Godot* made its English-language première. It caused a near-riot in the theatrical world, with audience members groaning and complaining that it was boring, offensive and impossible to like – which was sort of the point. It soon became recognised as a classic. In the 1980s Beckett was invited to Germany to direct a production of the play. Presented with the script he had not read in many years, he said of his masterpiece, 'This thing needs a good edit.'

SNOW WAY TO TREAT US

Snow Patrol may have formed at the University of Dundee, but four out of the five members are from Northern Ireland, so we'll claim them as one of ours. It was their major-label debut album, *Final Straw*, that shot them to superstardom, and it was released today in 2003. Since its release, the band has sold over ten million albums worldwide. They nearly didn't make it – they were dropped by their label in 2001. Happily, they channelled this disappointment into their breakthrough single, 'Run'.

HE REALLY PUT HIS HEART INTO HIS JOB

Heart-attack victims and screenwriters should today be proud of Dr Frank Pantridge of Hillsborough, Co. Down. This brilliant cardiologist invented the portable defibrillator while working at the Royal Victoria Hospital in Belfast, and told the world about it in *The Lancet* today in 1967. Since then the idea of treating victims before they get to hospital has saved millions of lives. The very first device weighed 154lb (70kg) and operated from car batteries. It was installed in a Belfast ambulance, making the city 'the safest place in the world to have a heart attack'.

PUNCHING ABOVE
HER WEIGHT

Very few athletes have the talent and charisma not just to become a winner but to champion their whole sport. Katie Taylor certainly has that gift. After making her Olympic debut in London today in 2012, she punched her way to a gold medal, becoming the first ever female lightweight Olympic champion. She also held the Irish, European and World titles, was an international soccer player and is pretty handy at Gaelic football. She's earned the respect not just of Ireland, but of sports fans and women across the globe. Fittingly she was named Sportsperson of the Year in 2012.

DEEPLY TALENTED

Has anyone done more to put a city on the map than Bindon Blood Stoney? Over 40 years, from 1859, this brilliant engineer from Co. Offaly transformed the port of Dublin. He devised an ingenious new way to extend the docks using huge blocks of pre-cast concrete. Each 350-ton monolith took four weeks to make, and was put in place using a diving bell of his design. This was still in use in the 1960s. Engineers came from around the world to marvel at Stoney's work. Dublin was now a deep-water port, and the city never looked back. As an encore, Stoney designed Grattan Bridge, O'Connell Bridge and Butt Bridge, which opened today in 1879.

EUROPE'S FINEST FARMYARD

A pastoral paradise reflecting Man's perfect harmony with Nature – well, that might be a bit over the top, but Larchill Arcadian Garden is certainly very beautiful. And this 'Ferme Ornée' (ornamental farm) is the only garden of its type in Europe. It's a working farm with exquisite follies, grottos, temples, statues, tree-lined avenues, lakes and a walled garden. It was rescued from ruin by an award-winning restoration project, and its 19th-century splendour was once again unveiled today in 1999.

A VERY BRIGHT MAN

Despite Streete, Co. Westmeath, being overcast for 250 days every year, from his observatory William Wilson became the first man to measure the temperature of the sun. His figure was 11,894°F (6,590°C) – not that far off the modern value of 10,967°F (6,075°C). In 1896 he photographed the bones in a man's arm, making him one of the first people in history to take an X-ray photograph. And today in 1898, Wilson took the first ever photograph of a sunspot.

OUR FATHER, WHO ART NOT IN HEAVEN...

You might think it sad that today in 1919, Father Pat Noise died when his carriage plunged into the River Liffey, as commemorated by the plaque on O'Connell Bridge. But the brass monument is a hoax, placed in the gap left by the control box for the 'Millennium Countdown' clock – the name is a play on 'pater noster' (our father). It was placed there in 2004, but no one noticed for two years. The council then tried to remove it, but people loved its daftness, so Father Noise's fake memorial is up there still, the only one of its kind.

FIRST MAN OF GERMANY

11 In the 1850s, Germany's industry was lagging far behind its rival England's – largely because it was cheaper to import coal than dig it out of local mines. Then Dublin-born engineer William Mulvany, organised the sinking of three new mines in 1856 – Hibernia, Shamrock and Erin – that exploited rich coal seams. These turned the Ruhr from a sleepy valley into the industrial powerhouse of Germany. Curiously, it was this increased industry that led to the uncovering of the first Neanderthal fossils in the area, today in 1856 – 'Neander' is the name of a nearby valley.

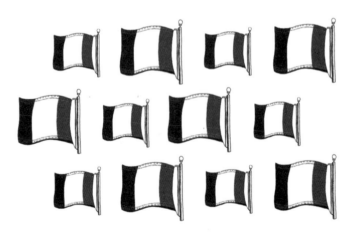

TICKET TO THE RIDES

12 All aboard! Today in 1846 saw the world's very first railway excursion organised for a sporting event, to the Curragh horse races on the new Great Southern and Western Railway. Bets on how late the thing would be were taken immediately. The service did prove popular, so much so that the course later had its very own siding that came off the mainline. Incidentally, it's fitting that the Curragh is the heartland of Irish racing – the name comes from the Irish word 'cuirreach', which literally means 'racecourse'.

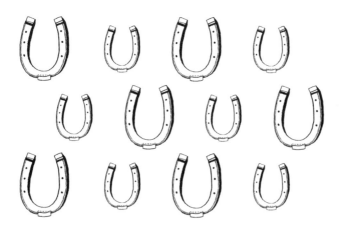

AUGUST

MY HEART'S RIGHT WHERE?

 Not everyone in the world knows where Tipperary is, but at least they know where they are relative to it: 'It's a Long Way to Tipperary' is the song that put the town on the map, or at least on the tips of everyone's tongues. Composer Jack Judge's family were from Co. Mayo, and his ditty was sung today in 1914 by the Connaught Rangers as they marched through Boulogne at the start of the First World War. It soon became popular with both sides, and famous worldwide as a music hall tune. It was originally called 'It's a long Way to Connemara'.

'BETCHA U2 ARE SHITTIN' THEMSELVES'

It was a fair old year for films, 1991, but the flick the world fell in love with was *The Commitments* (released today). From out of nowhere, the movie brought the soul of northside Dublin and earthy Irish humour to a grateful global audience. Voted best Irish film of all time in a 2005 poll, it was a springboard for a whole generation of Irish acting talent. It also launched the music career of four young siblings who were spotted at the audition but only had minor acting parts: Andrea, Sharon, Caroline and Jim, who became better known by their surnames – the Corrs.

OFF WITH ITS HEAD

Surely the world's unluckiest artist was Dublin-born sculptor JH Foley. He must have thought his career was going swimmingly as he bagged several commissions for high-ranking 19th century individuals, including Lord Carlisle, Lord Dunkellin and Field Marshal Gough. But with the creation of the Irish Free State, the artistic wind changed somewhat, and these same works were destroyed overnight: his statue of Lord Dunkellin was decapitated and dumped in the Galway River. However, Foley's talents live on in the Albert Memorial in London and the statue of Daniel O'Connell in Dublin (unveiled today in 1882).

UNDERSEA SUCCESS

With its quiet coves, scattered farms and dozing seals, Valentia Island in western Ireland might not seem much like the flashpoint of a global communications revolution. But the first transatlantic telegraph cable was laid from there to Heart's Content in eastern Newfoundland. The very first communications between the two continents went down the wire today in 1858. This was nothing short of fantastical at the time – messages that took ships ten days to deliver could now arrive in mere minutes.

OLD-FASHIONED SPORTSMANSHIP

Those ancient Greeks thought they were so clever, what with inventing the Olympic Games and all – and now it turns out that they didn't. A very similar event, the Tailteann Games, had been held in Ireland since at least 1600 BC – that's 1,000 years before the Greek events. The Tailteann was a cultural occasion, about honouring ancestors and passing laws, as well as running, jumping, throwing things, wrestling and racing horses. They were proudly revived at Croke Park in 1924, with two weeks of athletic endeavour that climaxed on this day. Fittingly, many Olympians who had competed in Paris took part, presumably not in the making-laws bit, though.

ELECTRON EQUALITY

George Johnstone Stoney, from Co. Offaly, introduced the concept of the electron as the 'fundamental unit quantity of electricity' today in 1874, and named it in 1891. This is pretty impressive, considering it would be several more years before JJ Thomson actually spotted the thing. Stoney also campaigned for higher education to be opened to women – thanks to him, women earned medical qualifications in Ireland long before their sisters in Britain.

CLIMB EVERY MOUNTAIN

John Tyndall, from Leighlinbridge, Co. Carlow, was a brilliant 19th-century scientist, who became known for his lively lectures. In a famous one at the Royal Institution, Tyndall demonstrated the total internal reflection of light in a stream of falling water. As well as being very pretty, this 'light fountain' was the scientific basis for modern fibre-optic technology. He also discovered the Greenhouse Effect and perfected the foghorn. In his holidays, Tyndall became one of the first people to climb the Weisshorn (today in 1861) and the Matterhorn in the Alps.

CROSSING OVER DOWN UNDER

Robert O'Hara Burke from Galway was an ex-police officer who led the first expedition to cross Australia from south to north. His party of 19 men, 27 camels and 23 horses set off on their 2,020-mile (3,250km) journey from Melbourne today, in 1860, across the then unknown interior of Australia. However, it soon became aware that Burke didn't know what the heck he was doing, and after 400 miles (644km) several people deserted. Just four men reached the north coast and Burke himself died on the way back. Only one man of the original party made it there and back – John King, another Irishman.

KNOCK, KNOCK, WHO'S THERE?

Around 8pm on this evening in 1879, a group of 15 men, women and children saw a vision of the Virgin Mary, Joseph and St John the Evangelist hovering elegantly by the south end of Knock parish church. Whether this was a genuine apparition, a hallucination or a canny strategy to bring in some tourist cash is unknowable. However, it's certain that Knock, Co. Mayo soon became a phenomenon on the scale of Lourdes, and today its National Shrine attracts hundreds of thousands of pilgrims from all over the world, every year.

DEAD BRILLIANT

Officially, it's Ireland's Natural History Museum, but everyone knows it as the Dead Zoo. Opened in Dublin today in 1857, to house one of the world's largest collections of deceased things, it has hardly changed at all, making it a 'museum of a museum'. It is unique in the world for the size (10,000+ exhibits) and the style of its collection – eccentric taxidermy, amusing group poses, and bullet holes often visible. When a new entrance was built in 1909, nobody could be bothered turning the whales, elephants and other big creatures around to face the new door – this is why you approach so many of the exhibits via their backsides.

PUNCH-DRUNK PADDY

23 Robert 'Paddy' Mayne from Co. Down was an Irishman whose thirst for violence was rivalled only by his thirst for Guinness. He became Irish Universities' Heavyweight Boxing Champion (today in 1936), was one of the most decorated soldiers on any side in the Second World War, and helped found the SAS. Mayne was also a fearsome international rugby player. During the 1938 Lions tour of South Africa, Paddy relaxed after games by 'wrecking hotels and fighting dockers'.

A DEAD GOOD INVENTION

24 The next time you see a movie assassin line up his kill shot in the crosshairs of his rifle sight, you can be proud that his murder is only possible thanks to Howard Grubb of Dublin. Today in 1901, he gave the world its first look at the reflector sight, which allows a reticle to be seen on the target without distortion by parallax – that is, when you wiggle your head about. It was far better than the iron sights of the day, and is still used on all kinds of weapons, from small firearms to fighter aircraft, including modern head-up displays.

COUNTESS WITH THE MOSTEST

A bit of Irish cheek and a heaving bosom can get a girl a long way – as Eliza Gilbert from Co. Sligo proved. She reinvented herself as 'Lola Montez, the Spanish dancer' on the London stage, and bounced upwards through society upon the beds of European men including Franz Liszt and Alexander Dumas. At a meeting with King Ludwig I of Bavaria, the monarch asked if her bosom was real – Lola promptly tore off enough of her top to prove the point. The 60-year-old Ludwig was a goner and today, in 1847, he made her a countess. For the next year the bossy madam practically ran Bavaria. Unsurprisingly, her main political contribution was a series of liberal reforms.

TOP TREASURE TURNS UP

When a peasant woman dug up a nice-looking ornament today in 1850 on Bettystown beach, Co. Meath, she can hardly have known the wonder of what she had unearthed. It was the Tara brooch, one of the finest examples of 7th-century metalworking anywhere in Europe. After being shown at London's Great Exhibition it also fuelled the boom in Celtic (or La Tene) art. Incidentally, she probably really dug it up inland – but the quick-thinking colleen fibbed to avoid a claim of ownership by the landlord.

DAWN OF THE EGG CHASERS

 Every sports fan knows that William Webb Ellis kicked off the game of rugby by running with the ball during a school football match. (The rules were drawn up today, in 1845.) But you may not be aware that Ellis's father was an army officer based in Ireland who often saw the game of caid being played. This Gaelic sport involves running with a ball to get it across a boundary with much physical contact. Some historians believe Ellis Jr was merely demonstrating in England the game he had learnt here.

PUKKA CHUKKA

 Considering the Irish love of horses, it's no surprise that one of our boys played a big role in creating the game of polo. A Tibetan version of the game is as old as the hills (or mountains in their case) – the local word for ball is 'pulu'. But it wasn't until the mid-19th century that an Irishman, Captain John Watson, freshly returned from India with the 13th Hussars cavalry, created the first set of written rules for playing the game. He was also part of the team that won the first ever international polo tournament, the Westchester Cup, today in 1886.

ELEVATED TO THE HIGHEST STATUS

Who needs cathedrals, skyscrapers or castles when you've got cranes? Belfast is rightly proud that its biggest and most famous landmarks are the twin gantry cranes, Samson and Goliath. They straddle the world's largest dry dock (1,824 x 305ft/556 x 93m) in what was once one of the biggest shipyards. Goliath stands 315ft (96m) high, while Samson is taller at 348ft (106m), and together they can lift over 1,600 tons, making them among the strongest cranes anywhere. And today in 1995, they were officially scheduled as historic monuments so no one can knock them down. I'd like to see them try...

ANYTHING YOU CAN DO...

Today in 1883, at the Monasterevan Athletic Sports, Pat Davin leapt 23ft 2in (7.06m) to claim the world long-jump record. It's not huge compared with the efforts of athletes today, but remarkable when you consider that Davin was leaping from grass, not off a board, and that at the time he was also the holder of the world high-jump record (6ft 2¾in/1.9m). Pat had taken that title off his brother. He is the only man in history to hold both high and long jump records.

MARY MAKES HER MARK

31 The fact that she died today in 1869 wasn't particularly great news for Mary Ward. However, the fact that she did so made her an Irish person of international repute. You see, Mary tumbled from an experimental steam car built by her cousins, and in doing so became the world's very first motor vehicle accident fatality.

SEPTEMBER

HAY FEVER

Forget online dating, Lisdoonvarna's matchmaking festival, Matchmaker Ireland, has been helping lovestruck couples cop off for more than 150 years.

It is Europe's largest matchmaking festival, and the normally tiny town in Co. Clare will swell with 40,000 heaving, hopeful bosoms. It's held in September because that was traditionally when all the crops were gathered in. When the hay was in the barn, lovers finally had something they could roll around in. And today in 2013 saw a new twist on old traditions, with the first ever LGBT matchmaking weekend.

DELIGHTED TO MEET YOU, HARUTIUN

Heard the one about the Armenian law student who fled persecution in Turkey, set up a sweet shop in Cork and became world-famous? Harutiun Batmazian arrived in Cork as an outcast – but although he had no English, he did know how to make bloody amazing sweets. He exhibited his wares at the Cork International Exhibition today in 1902, to lip-smacking delight. So he set up his sweet shop, Hadji Bey & Cie, which became an icon, supplying Buckingham Palace and Harrods in London, as well as Macy's and Bloomingdale's in New York. It's largely thanks to Harutiun that the western taste for Turkish Delight was established.

H₂0 IS GO

William Higgins was a brilliant but rather grumpy chemist from Collooney in Co. Sligo, who laid out much of atomic theory 19 years before the more famous John Dalton. The 26-year-old Higgins published his ideas about 'ultimate particles of elementary matter' today in 1789, showing how they combine or react to form compounds. It was Higgins who was the first to use letters to denote chemical elements, such as 'H' for hydrogen and 'O' for oxygen.

REELY SMART THINKING

Louis Brennan from Castlebar, Co. Mayo, noticed that if you pull thread from a cotton reel, the reel moves away. 'That's a fun way to amuse the cat,' would have been most people's reaction to that. But Brennan realised that if you put two reels of steel wire inside a torpedo you could propel and steer it from the shore. And so he created the world's first practical guided missile. The Brennan Torpedo, which he patented today in 1877, could hit a floating target up to 2,000 yards (1,829m) away at 27 knots and turn through 180 degrees to hit it from the side.

THE ORIGINAL MAD MAN

The star of perhaps the most famous and effective advertising poster in history was an Irishman. Horatio Kitchener, better known as Field Marshall Kitchener, was from Co. Kerry, and it was his face that appeared on the British 'Your Country Needs You!' recruitment poster during the First World War. It first appeared on a magazine cover today in 1914, and was quickly copied by other countries, including the US, Russia and Germany. Kitchener really should have thought twice about encouraging such an almighty punch-up, though – his ship was sunk by a German mine in 1916.

GRACE UNDER PRESSURE

Grace O'Malley was a 16th-century clan chieftain and ferocious pirate of the seas off the coast of Co. Mayo. She led a crew that terrorised the fishing boats and she soon had a fleet of ships and a great deal of land. When the English governor tried to stop her antics by taking her sons hostage, O'Malley demanded an audience with Queen Elizabeth I. Incredibly, this she got, today in 1593. Grace must have been quite the charmer, because far from flinging O'Malley out on her ear, or indeed having that ear removed from her body along with the rest of her head, Elizabeth agreed to her demands. Apparently the ladies chatted in Latin, as O'Malley spoke no English and Elizabeth spoke no Irish.

A GEM OF A PHRASE

As one of the first doctors to advocate inoculation against smallpox, William Drennan from Belfast deserves a proud mention here. He was also a great proponent of 'washing your flaming hands when you're told' to prevent infection. But it's for his poem *When Erin First Rose*, published today in 1795, that he truly goes down in history – it's the first-ever description of Ireland as the 'Emerald Isle'.

SEPTEMBER

HIS IDEAS WERE PURE SPECULATION

Given the state of the economy, it's kind of fitting that a highly indebted Irishman addicted to property speculation came up with the concept of the entrepreneur. Richard Cantillon from Co. Kerry founded France's Banque Générale and made a fortune by fuelling a speculative land bubble via his own monopoly on notes. He also wrote a famous *Essai* (published today in 1755) that is considered the first complete treatise on economics. This influenced Adam Smith and other famous economists, and introduced the term, entrepreneur. Wish he hadn't bothered...

TANKS FOR YOUR HARD WORK

War – and action movies – would never be the same after Walter Wilson got involved. The engineer and inventor from Blackrock, Co. Dublin led the project that produced the first tank prototype in history. Nicknamed 'Little Willie', this vehicle made its first test run today in 1915. Wilson was acting on the commission of Winston Churchill, who wanted an armoured vehicle that could repel missiles, protect passengers and negotiate the wildly uneven surface of no man's land – i.e. something that would get him down Pearse Street in a hurry.

THE THINGS SHE DID FOR HER COUNTRY

Examine an Irish banknote issued from today in 1928 until 1975 and you'll see a female personification of Ireland on one side. This famous image was created by the brilliant painter Sir John Lavery, but the model he chose as the ultimate Irishwoman was actually his American wife, Hazel. Still, although she might not have come from this country, she certainly had a real passion for all things Irish. Patriotic Lady Lavery had affairs with both Kevin O'Higgins and Michael Collins.

LOOKS CAN BE DECEIVING – WE HOPE

So, you're making a film in Ireland because it's cheap and we're good at it, but you have a problem – your story is set somewhere else. Don't worry! Our landscape has a long history of doubling for other parts of the world on screen: Temple Bar played Boston in *Far and Away*; Trinity College stood in for Liverpool University in *Educating Rita*; Co. Kildare played Scotland in *Braveheart*; and Ballinesker Beach in Co. Wexford played Normandy in the famous battle scene at the start of *Saving Private Ryan* (released today in 1998).

SEPTEMBER

TOP IN HIS FIELD

'The mad mechanic' was how neighbours described Harry Ferguson from Growell, Co. Down, but he later showed them he wasn't all that daft when he revolutionised farming. Ferguson's brainwave was to couple a plough to a tractor via a rigid three-point linkage (he got the first of many patents today, in 1917). The plough added drag force on the rear wheels, thereby providing traction and manoeuvrability. Three-point linkage soon became the industry standard worldwide, and his name lives on in the tractor firm Massey Ferguson. Harry was also the first Irish man to fly, in a plane of his own design.

PRO-CREATION

With an area of over 2 acres (0.8ha) and with 120 rooms, Tullynally Castle, Co. Westmeath is the largest in Ireland. Despite its dimensions, it became the first castle in Europe to have central heating, today in 1790. This was thanks to Irish inventor Richard Edgeworth, who installed a pioneering system. Edgeworth invented many ingenious devices, including one that could measure a plot of land, an optical telegraph system and an early caterpillar track. This gentleman was prolific in everything he did – he somehow found time to father 22 children.

THERE'S NOTHING QUIET ABOUT HER

Maureen O'Hara was an actress and singer from Ranelagh in Dublin who made five films with her great friend John Wayne. Perhaps her best loved was *The Quiet Man* (released today, in 1952), which was filmed on the west coast of Ireland. O'Hara cornered the movie market in feisty passionate heroines and while some people say the hot-tempered, flame-haired Irish lass image is a cliché, we all know they're one of our proudest national achievements.

COMPUTERS FROM CORK

The mathematician George Boole was born in England, but when he was made Professor of Mathematics at Queen's College, Cork in 1849, something in the Irish air appeared to inspire him. For it was here that he did his most famous work, publishing his book *An Investigation of the Laws of Thought* today in 1854. This laid down what is now known as Boolean algebra, a form of logic that became the basis of the modern digital computer. In effect, Boole pretty much founded the field of computer science.

JB SPORTS

Talk about playing people into a corner – Jonah Barrington was an Irish judge who wrote some withering, brutally funny memoirs that got the legal and political personalities of his time fuming. They were published today, in 1827, and just three years later Barrington became the only judge to be forcibly removed from office by both Houses of Parliament. Curiously, Jonah Barrington is also the name of another great Irishman, the superlative squash player who won six British Open titles between 1967 and 1973.

THE EYES HAVE IT

You know when you can't see something for looking? Opthalmologist Arthur Jacob from Knockfin, Co. Laois took that to a whole new level. Jacob was a brilliant medic who founded the Dublin Medical Press and the City of Dublin Hospital today in 1832. But it was his discovery in 1819 that really marked his place in history. He announced the discovery of a previously unknown membrane of the eye that forms the retina (now known as *membrana Jacobi*), which is remarkable considering it had been literally right in front of the eyes of centuries of doctors.

LIGHTING UP TIME

18 Which mighty metropolis was the first in the world to be lit by electricity – Dublin? London? New York? No, it was Birr, Co. Offaly (population 5,818), today in 1879. The 4th Earl of Rosse was just one of a great line of ingenious aristocrats, and he installed a waterwheel that turned a turbine that supplied electricity to Birr Castle and the nearby town. Also of interest, but perhaps not of so much use, the Earl devised an accurate way of measuring the temperature of the Moon.

COCOA'S A GO-GO

19 When physician Hans Sloane from Killyleagh, Co. Down, left for Jamaica today in 1687, he was embarking on a voyage that would bring him wealth and bring us something we wish we didn't like so much. In the Caribbean he studied many animals and plants, one of which was cocoa. Sloane found it, frankly, disgusting. But after a bit of experimentation he found that mixing it with milk made it less sickening. On his return he sold this as a medicine, before it gained popularity as a drink. His patented recipe made him rich during his lifetime and, in the 19th century, Sloane's was the first chocolate brand produced by Cadbury.

GET LOST

20 It took 1,000 local people three years to design and plant the Peace Maze in Castlewellan Forest Park, Co. Down, which opened today in 2001. But it was worth it – the labyrinth's 6,000 yew trees enclosed over 2 miles (3.2km) of pathway covering 3 acres (1.2ha), and in 2004 it was recognised as the largest and longest maze in the world. Incidentally, it's called the Peace Maze because it represents the path to a peaceful future for Northern Ireland, not because once you've solved it you'll be too tired to fight anybody.

SATISFACTION GUARANTEED

21 Next time you stroll round your local department store, be proud of Timothy Eaton from Ballymena, Co. Antrim. After emigrating to Canada he founded Eaton's department store, and changed the face of shopping forever. He made ground-breaking innovations in the way we shop: first, all goods had one price – no haggling and no credit; and second, all purchases had a money-back guarantee. His final innovation was producing the world's first department-store mail-order catalogue (today in 1884). Each year, the new catalogue was a godsend to rural communities, as the old one was to rural lavatories.

ARE WE THERE YETI?

At 22,000ft (6,707m) up Mount Everest today in 1921, Col. Charles Howard-Bury from Co. Offaly was leading a reconnaissance expedition. This helped lay the groundwork for future climbing attempts, including the one by George Mallory in 1924, which may have reached the summit (Mallory was with Bury's party in 1921). Howard-Bury also found many footprints at high altitude, which he assumed were those of a wolf. But when his Sherpas insisted they were the tracks of a 'metch kangmi' ('filthy snowman'), this was mistranslated and a new phrase was coined – the Yeti has been known as the 'abominable snowman' ever since.

SEPTEMBER

THE SOLE OF DISCRETION

 One of the most unusual incidents in international diplomacy was proudly presided over by an Irishman, today in 1960. The Philippine delegate was speaking to the UN General Assembly about Soviet abuses of civil rights in Eastern Europe, when suddenly an enraged Nikita Khrushchev, the Soviet leader, began bellowing insults in Russian and pounding his fists on his desk. The Assembly President, Irish diplomat Frederick Boland, was too gobsmacked to restore order. The Assembly was therefore treated to the sight of Khrushchev becoming so irate that he removed his shoe and started banging it on the desk.

OYSTER'S BIG OPENING

 How to get a few more punters into his Galway hotel now summer was over – that was the problem facing manager Brian Collins today in 1954. His solution was to hold a banquet of oysters, which had just come into season. Then just 34 guests, mostly locals, enjoyed a few dozen oysters each. Today the event pulls in over 22,000 visitors a year, who sink tons of the famous native oysters. It's the world's oldest oyster festival, and the most internationally recognised Irish festival after St Patrick's Day. The UK's *Sunday Times* newspaper rated it as one of the 12 greatest shows on Earth.

THE BIGGEST SCHOOL BAND IN THE WORLD

Everyone knows this is a musical island, but we really do have the best and the biggest. U2 have sold more than 150 million records worldwide, but the band began humbly today in 1976, when 14-year-old Larry Mullen Jr posted a note on the board at Mount Temple Comprehensive School asking for musicians. Six people showed up to rehearsals in his kitchen: among them were David Evans (The Edge), Adam Clayton and Paul Hewson (Bono). They decided on their band name as the 'least bad' of the suggestions put forward. Bono got his from a hearing-aid shop.

MIKE'S FULL OF HOT AIR

If you'd visited New Castle House in Ballymahon, Co. Longford today, in 1971, you'd have seen a handful of hot air balloons drifting serenely overhead. This was the very first Irish Hot Air Ballooning Championships – in fact, it was the first national ballooning championships anywhere in the world. The event is still running today, making it the oldest of its type. Now, though, the 'Irish Meet' is a much grander affair with dozens of balloon teams from all over the world taking part.

SEPTEMBER

HE PUTT THEM IN THEIR PLACE

 The Limerick-born broadcaster Terry Wogan began his career at Raidió Teilifís Éireann presenting *Jackpot* in the 1960s, before making his first BBC broadcast today in 1966. His lyrical but cynical commentary of the Eurovision Song Contest was the sole reason many British people watch the BBC coverage. Wogan highlights include referring to the hosts of the 2001 contest in Denmark, Søren Pilmark and Natasja Crone Back, as 'Doctor Death and the Tooth Fairy' for no good reason, and calling a Dutch presenter an 'eejit'. He also holed the longest golf putt ever seen on TV (33 yards/30.1m) in a 1981 pro-am at Gleneagles.

DONE WITH DUNG

 It wasn't so much a lack of horses (or elephants) that led Irish cycling legend RJ Mecredy to invent bicycle polo in 1891, more a love of all things bike-related. Mecredy was the first man to win a cycle race on pneumatic tyres (Dunlop's) and in 1890 he won all four English cycling championships. So this new sport made total sense. More so when the first international match was played at London's Crystal Palace today in 1901 – Ireland thrashed England 10–5.

THE ART OF CRIME

Russborough House in Co. Wicklow is not just the longest house in Ireland (its front is longer than two soccer pitches), it was also the venue for FOUR of the world's greatest art robberies. An IRA gang got the ball rolling in 1974 by pinching 19 Old Masters worth £8 million – then the single biggest art heist of all time – but the pictures were recovered. In May 1986, Martin Cahill had a pop, scooping even more – £30m worth. Most were recovered. Then two paintings were pinched in a 2001 ram-raid. They were also recovered, unfortunately just two days before five more were stolen, today in 2002.

YOU'VE GOT TO FIGHT FOR YOUR RIGHTS

As the son of WB Yeats' feisty muse Maud Gonne and republican John MacBride, Sean MacBride was never going to be a wallflower. But it's remarkable how much he accomplished in the pursuit of international human rights during the 1950s, 1960s and 1970s. He helped found Amnesty International (today in 1962) and served as its International Chairman. He was also Assistant Secretary-General of the United Nations, Chairman of UNESCO and winner of the Nobel Peace Prize in 1974, and the Lenin Peace Prize the year after.

OCTOBER

THE NAME'S MELVILLE, WILLIAM MELVILLE

With his upper-class accent, club membership, pipe and Savile Row suits, James Bond's boss 'M' is surely the picture of the quintessential Englishman – except that he was really Irish. William Melville, from Sneem, Co. Kerry, joined the Metropolitan Police in 1872 and soon proved a natural snooper. He worked his way up through Special Branch and eventually led the British government to form the Secret Service Bureau (formed today in 1909). This originally had 19 military intelligence departments, but only MI5 and MI6 still exist (apparently). Melville's codename was 'M', from his surname, a fact that later inspired author Ian Fleming.

THE GREENEST OF FINGERS

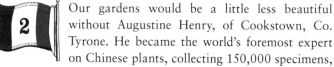

Our gardens would be a little less beautiful without Augustine Henry, of Cookstown, Co. Tyrone. He became the world's foremost expert on Chinese plants, collecting 150,000 specimens, and discovering 500 new species and 25 genera. Many familiar garden plants bear his name. He was the only westerner who knew where the holy grail for nurserymen – the handkerchief tree – could be found. And happily for fruit cocktail fans, it was Henry who, today in 1899, pointed collector EH Wilson in the direction of the Chinese gooseberry, now known as the kiwi fruit.

POTTINGER'S EASTERN PROMISE

Travelling across Asia disguised as a Muslim merchant to study local languages was just the start of the adventures of Henry Pottinger from Co. Down (born today, in 1789). As a soldier he led an expedition into the wild unknown lands between Belujistan and Persia, a journey so dangerous that no other European would attempt it for 100 years. While working as an administrator, he managed to wangle a promising but totally undeveloped island from China, and in 1843 became the first Governor of this hopeful little outpost. Thus Pottinger pretty much established modern Hong Kong.

A CUT BELOW THE REST

Beautiful linen is what first made Banbridge in Co. Down famous – it was once the biggest production centre in Ireland, with 26 bleach greens along the river. But it really drives its way into the history books for an innovative bit of civil engineering. The town's main street was so steep that horses used to keel over when they pulled wagons up it. So in 1834 the engineer William Dargan built 'Downshire Bridge', also known as 'The Cut', which is now recognised as the world's first underpass. Traffic first passed through on this day, and the first graffiti was probably put up about three hours later.

THINKING PINK

Film comedy would be a lot poorer if wasn't for Anthony 'Tony' Adams from Carbury, Co. Kildare. The film and theatrical producer oversaw the creation of many of writer/director Blake Edwards's movies, including six *Pink Panther* films, *Victor/Victoria* and the raunchy classic *10*, featuring Dudley Moore and Bo Derek, which bounced onto our screens for the first time today in 1979.

RADICAL, MAN

John Toland was an Irish radical far ahead of his time. He wrote over 100 books, most of which ragged on the church. His most famous work was *Christianity Not Mysterious* (published today in 1696), in which Toland challenged not just church leadership, but all unquestioned authority. His enemies soon cast him a dangerous radical, but he was the first person to be called a 'freethinker'. His radical views included the wild notion that liberty was a defining characteristic of what it means to be human. Toland thought that political institutions should guarantee freedom, not just maintain order. Craziness, clearly.

THE LAST LAUGH

Rebellious, lyrical, unpredictable and barking mad – you can certainly see the Irishness in the humour of comedy legend Spike Milligan. Born of Irish parents and later in life an Irish citizen (today in 1962), Milligan co-created the hugely influential *The Goon Show*. This launched Peter Sellers as a star and created a new sort of comedy – without *The Goon Show* there would have been no Peter Cook, Monty Python and even The Beatles cited their surrealism as a big influence. On Milligan's gravestone is the Irish inscription, 'Dúirt mé leat go raibh mé breoite', which translates as 'I told you I was ill.'

FORD'S FOOTBALL FACTORY

If you've ever got stuck behind a tractor on a country road, you won't be surprised to hear that Ireland once had the biggest tractor factory in the world. When Ford's Model F tractor debuted today in 1917, it soon did for farm machinery what the Model T had done for road vehicles. Henry Ford's father was from Cork and he decided to build all his tractors in Ireland. At its peak, there were 7,000 workers in Cork's huge riverside plant. The factory soccer team even won the Football Association of Ireland Cup in 1926 – a competition now fittingly sponsored by Ford.

ROAD TO NOWHERE

Construction work on the N18 route in Co. Clare ground to a halt today in 1999. The reason? A fairy tree lying in the path of the upgraded road. And everyone knows it's bad luck to destroy one of those. The locals duly kicked up a fuss and eventually the powers-that-don't-be-as-much-as-they-think relented. 'Only in Ireland!' some may scoff. But surely it's nicer to live in a world where motorways are moved, just a wee bit, at the insistence of the people, to make way for fairy trees?

PEOPLE OF PEACE

10 From one specific tragedy came the flowering of a broader hope. Outraged by the deaths of three children in a Troubles-related incident, Betty Williams and Mairead Corrigan from Belfast became leaders of a virtually spontaneous mass movement – Peace People. Suddenly 35,000 people of all political and religious backgrounds were marching for an end to violence. And today in 1977, their spirit was recognised with the Nobel Prize for Peace. It was an inspiring moment for Ireland and the wider world. Aged just 32, Corrigan was then the youngest-ever Nobel Peace Prize laureate.

IT'S ALL IN THE WRIST

11 Abraham Colles was a brilliant surgeon from Kilkenny, who became President of the Royal College of Surgeons of Ireland aged just 28, and led it to become one of most respected medical institutions in Europe. He also went down in history for accurately describing one of the most common types of broken wrist (Colles' fracture), in a paper today in 1814. His observations were years ahead of their time, being published long before X-rays were invented.

WHAT IS SHE DOING WITH THOSE COCONUTS?

According to some sources, the first European actually to step onto New World territory on this day in 1492 was not Christopher Columbus, but an Irish member of his crew, Patrick Maguire. There were several Irish hands on board the *Santa Maria*. Whether Maguire did this out of bravery, to protect his captain, or because the girls of the native Arawak tribe were standing naked on the beach, we cannot be sure.

IRELAND WINS BY A NOSE

No wonder Ireland is horse-daft – National Hunt racing began here. In fact, the 'steeplechase' was born when Edmund Blake and Cornelius O'Callaghan raced their horses between the steeples of the churches in Buttevant and Doneraile in Co. Cork today in 1752. They tore along the banks of the Awbeg River at breakneck speed, clearing whatever obstacles the landscape threw in their way – stone walls, ditches, hedges and passed-out spectators.

A DUBLIN DEBUT

The 16-year-old American boy strode into the Gate Theatre in Dublin and announced that he was the 'Star of the New York Theatre Guild'. The manager knew fine well that he wasn't anything of the sort, but there was something in the kid's delivery, so he gave him a part as the evil Duke Alexander in the upcoming play *Jew Suss*. The play earned good reviews when it opened tonight, in 1931. The lad stayed for the rest of the season, later playing Claudius and the Ghost in *Hamlet*. His name was Orson Welles, and a remarkable career had just been launched.

OPEN MIND, OPEN HOUSE

There would have been no William Butler Yeats without Sir Samuel Ferguson. This poet had a passion for Gaelic mythology that paved the way for the other poets of the Irish Literary Revival. He wrote many of his poems with both Irish and English translations. Ferguson's seminal work, the long poem *Congal*, was first published today in 1872. His house in North Great George's St, Dublin, was open to everyone interested in art, literature or music. Which you might think would pull in half the population of the country, particularly if he was laying on cake.

OCTOBER

MENTAL ARITHMETIC

'Balls, I think I've left the gas on!' or 'Ooh, I fancy a pie for tea,' are thoughts that might pop into most of our heads as we go for a stroll. But here's what dropped into William Rowan Hamilton's brain by the Royal Canal in Dublin today, in 1843: $i^2 = j^2 = k^2 = ijk = -1$.

Don't worry, we're baffled as well. But apparently this was the invention of quaternions, a Big Thing in maths. He carved the equation into the side of nearby Broome Bridge with his penknife (the vandal) and today it's vital to computer graphics and manoeuvring spacecraft. And don't feel inadequate – Hamilton was so brilliant he could also read 13 languages.

GUESS HE DIDN'T WATCH MUCH TELLY

George Bernard Shaw is one of Ireland's true literary heavyweights. He's also one of the people who makes you wonder what the hell you're doing with your life: he wrote five novels, 63 plays, dozens of stories and essays, 250,000 letters, is the only person ever to have been awarded both a Nobel Prize in Literature and an Academy Award – and he also helped found the London School of Economics, today in 1895.

HOME AT LAST

18 Some people see the world's great sights, places and people that this world has to offer, and then choose Ireland. Take film director John Huston – after a glittering Hollywood career he chose to become an Irish citizen in 1964. He travelled the world, directing 37 films, including classics such as *The Maltese Falcon* (released today in 1941), *The Treasure of the Sierra Madre*, *The African Queen* and *The Man Who Would Be King*. But he finally settled in Craughwell, Co. Galway, where he became Master of Fox Hounds of the local hunt.

I DON'T CARE WHAT THEY'RE CALLED, JUST STOP PLAYING THEM

19 The uilleann pipes are the national bagpipe of Ireland and a rousing part of any hoolie, which is all well and good. But they also deserve worldwide recognition for being the pipes that sound least like a bag of mad cats being tied to an ambulance, being notably sweeter and quieter than the Scottish instrument. They were only given the name by music scholar Grattan Flood, today in 1911, when he mistranslated the expression 'woollen pipes' in Shakespeare's *The Merchant of Venice*, back into Irish: 'union pipes' is the older name.

PRIESTLY PRODUCTION LINE

You might have thought there would be priests all over the show in the 18th century, but actually there was a shortage. So St Patrick's College, Maynooth, Co. Kildare, was founded in 1795 as a seminary to produce some home-grown holy men. And we got good – by 1850 it was the largest seminary in the world. Since then it has got even bigger, with a magnificent chapel founded today in 1875. It has now ordained more than 11,000 priests. Alas, like many of our greatest products these days, we have exported most of those.

RESISTANCE IS (NOT) FUTILE

To cut the outrageous rents being charged by landlords, the Irish Land League was founded today in 1879. This unleashed a 'Land War', but the League didn't back down. To say the resistance was a success is an understatement. Rents were reduced and eventually an Act of Parliament in 1903 allowed tenant farmers to buy out their freeholds. By 1914, 75 per cent of occupiers were buying their farms. This wasn't just important for Irish farmers – the League inspired other successful movements around the world. And Gandhi took note of the League's proclamation of non-violent protest.

MAYOR PLAYER

Life wasn't plain sailing for William Russell Grace, but he certainly found safe harbour in the end. Grace fled Co. Cork at the height of the potato famine before finding lowly work in Peru. Eventually, though, he made a fortune in the shipping business and became a philanthropist. Thanks to his huge donations to Irish famine relief, he was nominated as the first ever Catholic Mayor of New York today in 1880, and served two terms. It was Grace who accepted France's gift of the Statue of Liberty, and his firm owned one of the first commercial vessels to sail through the Panama Canal.

THE UNIVERSE IS USSHERED INTO EXISTENCE

A brilliant scholar but a somewhat eccentric theologian, James Ussher was the Archbishop of Armagh and Primate of All Ireland. He got it into his head that by working backwards through all the years and lifespans given in the Bible he could work out an accurate chronology of the book. He could then calculate the exact day that God brought Creation into being. This turned out to be the night preceding Sunday 23 October, 4004 BC. So now you know.

JOINT HONOURS

Who says that cannabis makes you lethargic? William O'Shaughnessy from Limerick was a big fan, and he achieved a fair few things. Fresh out of medical school, he showed that cholera victims needed rehydrating with saline, laying the foundation for intravenous fluid therapy. He then moved to India, where he oversaw the installation of Asia's telegraph system, with 5,000 miles (8,047km) of cable. But one of his most important breakthroughs was in publicising the medicinal use of cannabis in a paper today in 1839. The drug was virtually unheard of in Europe at the time, and O'Shaughnessy became one of its most vocal supporters.

OCTOBER

HELL ON EARTH

No, not Grafton Street on a Saturday afternoon, but a cave on Station Island in Lough Derg, Co. Donegal. St Patrick was once there, looking for a way to inspire his followers, when Christ appeared and told him that this was the entrance to Hell itself. The followers were duly astonished. Useful in a tight spot, was Jesus. The site is now known as St Patrick's Purgatory and is a famous place of pilgrimage. The cave was closed up today in 1632, and has been blocked off ever since. Which is probably a good thing – you know, just in case.

THE TIME TRAVELLER'S RIDE OF CHOICE

With its stainless-steel body, gull-wing doors and sleek lines, there was a time when the DeLorean DMC-12 was the ultimate American sports car. But this iconic dream-machine actually rolled off a production line in Dunmurry, Northern Ireland, which produced 9,000 of the cool cars before DeLorean went bust in 1982. Of course, the car is most famous for being able to travel in time, which it first did today in 1985, with Marty McFly at the wheel…

THE SOUND OF THE FUTURE

The world can thank *The Bell Magazine* (first published in Dublin today in 1940) for discovering the greats of modern Irish writing. This monthly magazine of literature and social comment had a seminal influence on a generation of Irish creative life. Under the editorship of Seán Ó Faoláin, it was an outspoken liberal voice, fiercely critical of censorship, Gaelic revivalist ideology, clericalism and general stuck-upness. *The Bell* rang the changes for new writers such as Michael MacLaverty, Thomas Kinsella, Brendan Behan, Patrick Kavanagh, Patrick Swift and Conor Cruise O'Brien.

SWIFT THINKS BIG – AND SMALL

'Travels into Several Remote Nations of the World, in Four Parts, by Lemuel Gulliver, first a surgeon, and then a captain of several ships' isn't the catchiest of book titles, and the world knows it better as *Gulliver's Travels*. This satirical classic of literature by Dublin-born Jonathan Swift was first published today in 1726, and has never been out of print. As well as being a terrific read, the book coined the terms 'Lilliputian' and 'Yahoo', and described the orbits of the moons of Mars about 150 years before their actual discovery.

BALLS TO THE ENGLISH

 Along with neat lawns and cucumber sandwiches, you might think that the game of croquet was introduced to Ireland by the English aristocracy, but actually the reverse is true. An article published today in 1864 proved that the game was played in 1834 in Kingstown, 20 years before it was ever seen in England. Of course, the early Irish version was probably full contact and played with spiked clubs...

WOMAN 2 WOMAN

When Mary McAleese was voted President of Ireland today in 1997, it was a world first: never before, anywhere, had one female president replaced another. A proud day for Irish women indeed. Mind you, the odds of this happening were pretty good – four out of the five election candidates were women.

NOT A PUMPKIN IN SIGHT

Is Halloween becoming more Americanised these days? Well, Ireland has long had its own distinctive tradition on this day. Samhain ('sow-un') is the Celtic festival celebrating the start of winter, or the darker half of the year. Spirits of the dead abound on this night, and so the traditions of guising (to fool the spirits), lantern-carving and playing pranks began. And trick-or-treating came from the practice of collecting food for Samhain feasts. So Halloween has actually become more Irish over the years!

NOVEMBER

FOR PEAT'S SAKE

1 If there's one thing Ireland is good at, it's bogs – and that's official. Today in 1998, saw the opening of the Ballycroy National Park in Co. Mayo. This is not just the country's largest national park, but it also has the biggest stretch of blanket bog in Europe (46 sq. miles/119sq. km). Stick that in your fire and smoke it.

BURKITT FIGHTS BACK AGAINST CANCER

When Denis Burkitt from Enniskillen moved to Uganda, he simply wanted to bring medical help to poor people in remote areas. He ended up alerting science to a new type of cancer, now known as Burkitt's lymphoma, in a paper published today, in 1958. On the positive side, it was later discovered that this could be fully cured by chemotherapy, the only cancer that could at the time. This was a major breakthrough in cancer treatment. Burkitt also wrote a book, *Don't Forget Fibre in Your Diet*, which did wonders for bowel cancer prevention, and probably sales of Shredded Wheat, too.

IS IT A BOAT, IS IT A PLANE?
NO IT'S A PILE OF GLUE AND PLASTIC

If you've ever gone on holiday in a jet, you couldn't have done it without the technical wizardry of Shorts in Belfast. This firm was the first in the world to make production aircraft, when it formed back on this day in 1908, and today it's still a major manufacturer of nacelles, control systems and other bits and pieces that planes need to stop falling out of the sky. They also made the Second World War flying boats that were pretty cool but an absolute bastard to make as an Airfix model.

BELL'S SET RINGING

Many of us come up with theories about the physical world, but they're usually about things like why the supermarket queue you join is ALWAYS the slowest. John Bell from Belfast, however, was working at a different level. Today in 1964, he proved that some particles, even when separated by light years, can behave in a related way, for no discernible reason: a bit like identical twins both independently deciding to like Mumford & Sons. Explaining this further is beyond us, but let's just say that another very smart particle physicist has called Bell's theorem 'the most profound discovery of science'. So there you go.

WATER GENIUS

When Belfast-born William Mulholland arrived in Los Angeles in 1877 it had 9,000 inhabitants. Largely thanks to his efforts, by the time he died in 1935 there were 1.5 million. Mulholland was the engineering brains behind the 233 mile (375km) aqueduct, the longest in the world, which opened today in 1913. It brought water to arid LA from the Owens Valley, allowing it to grow into the second largest city in the US. Mulholland is also remembered in the eponymous Drive, one of the most famous roads in Hollywood and home to dozens of movie stars.

THE FANATICAL FRIAR

The east end of Glasgow was a fearsome place in 1870. The packed slums were racked with disease and the people crippled by poverty. To this hellhole was posted Brother Walfrid, born Andrew Kerins in Ballymote, Co. Sligo, whose spiritual mission was to help the poor as best he could. To keep youngsters out of the alehouses, Brother Walfrid turned to the new craze of football. He gathered some friends together in St Mary's church hall in Calton, Glasgow today in 1887, and formed the bones of a threadbare team. He named it after his roots – Celtic.

WHO THE HELL VOTED FOR BUTLER?

When Al Gore got more votes than George Bush today in 2000, but still lost the US Presidency, many blamed the unfair, nonsensical and overly complicated Electoral College system. Well, they should really have blamed it on Irishman Pierce Butler. He emigrated from Co. Carlow to South Carolina and became state legislator. It was his idea to have the President elected not directly by the voters but by 'electors', voted for state-by-state. And to be fair, his motivation for this was to avoid in-groups of powerful politicians skewing matters to favour their own candidates. So that worked well then.

THE ART OF SITTING ON YOUR ARSE

The Bibendum chair was unlike anything anybody had ever seen, let alone sat in, when Eileen Gray designed it. And it still looks futuristic today, nearly 100 years later. Gray was a pioneering modernist designer from Co. Wexford, whose designs were largely overlooked after the Second World War, until an auction on this day in 1972 showcased some of her work and shot her back into the limelight. She created several modern furniture classics, including the catchily named E1027 table, which was inspired by her sister's fondness for eating in bed. In 2009 a Gray armchair set a record for 20th-century decorative art by selling for €21.9 million.

BIG CAT'S BIG BREAK

The very first lion to appear in the MGM movie company's logo was Irish. Well, he was born at Dublin Zoo. Called 'Slats', he was somewhat lazier than the six other lions that have played the role, merely sitting there and looking around a bit, rather than doing any actual roaring. Still, he was impressive enough to keep the job for four years after making his debut today in 1924, before the film *He Who Gets Slapped*, starring Lon Chaney.

RECORD-SETTING BEAVER

10 A gent by the unlikely name of Hugh Beaver was entertaining some friends, today in 1951, by attempting to blast grouse out of the skies above North Slob, by the River Slaney. Sadly for them (the men, not the birds), the grouse proved too swift of wing. So much so that Hugh began wondering just which game bird, the golden plover or the grouse, could fly the fastest. The party was divided on the issue, and all subsequent researches drew a blank. Hugh realised there were more such questions being argued over, so he commissioned a volume of facts. This went on to become the world's best-selling copyrighted book ever, and is named after the company that Hugh was director of – Guinness World Records.

INSANELY STEEP

11 When it comes to cliffs, Ireland is, ahem, up there. Towering 2,257ft (688m) over the Atlantic breakers on the west of Co. Mayo are the precipices of Croaghaun, some of the highest sea cliffs in Europe. The Cliffs of Moher in Co. Clare are smaller, at 702ft (214m), but their sheer cragginess is mightily impressive. They were Ireland's biggest tourist draw in 2006, with one million visitors, and are also pretty good at acting: they famously doubled as the Cliffs of Insanity in the movie *The Princess Bride*, released today in 1987.

THE CRYSTAL THAT REALLY CUTS IT

12 When George and William Penrose started making flint glass in 1783, their talents soon made their town synonymous with exquisite crystal – Waterford. Production may now have moved elsewhere, but you can still see beautiful examples of Irish glassmaking at the French and German Grand Prix – the winners' trophies are Waterford crystal. And today in 2008 saw the unveiling of the new 12ft (3.7m) wide, 11,875lb (5,386kg) ball that drops in New York's Times Square on New Year's eve. It is covered in 2,668 brilliant crystals made here.

I SWEAR THAT'S BRILLIANT

13 Many people think that the first-ever use of the F-word on television was by English theatre critic Kenneth Tynan, today in 1965. But the plaudits should really go to the heroically honest Belfast man who painted the railings on Stranmillis Embankment alongside the River Lagan, who in 1959 told Ulster TV's teatime magazine programme, *Roundabout*, that his job was 'fucking boring'.

A SHINING WIT

'In Ireland the inevitable never happens and the unexpected constantly occurs.' So said the Reverend Sir John Pentland Mahaffy, and he was pretty much on the money. Mahaffy was a brilliant polymath who wrote definitive textbooks on pretty much any subject he chose to – from Egyptology to music. At a time when tongues were particularly sharp, he was regarded as one of Dublin's greatest wits. He even showed the young Oscar Wilde how to be droll – Wilde described Mahaffy as his 'first and greatest teacher'. While hoping to become Provost of Trinity College, Mahaffy heard that the incumbent was ill and remarked, 'Nothing trivial, I hope?' He finally got the job today in 1914.

BEING A TREE SUCKS

Lie beneath a leafy tree on a warm summer's day and most of us wouldn't be wondering about how sap gets up to the tree's leaves against the force of gravity. But then we aren't brilliant biologists like Henry Horatio Dixon of Dublin. Today in 1894, he pointed out that the sap is pulled upwards by a form of intermolecular attraction. Until then everyone wrongly believed it was pumped up from the roots.

BARRY LICKS LEPROSY

In a lab deep in Trinity College, Dublin, Dr Vincent Barry and his research team created a new drug, Clofazimine, in a bid to beat tuberculosis. It didn't help TB, but today in 1960 it was trialled on leprosy patients, with miraculous results. The drug is now part of a treatment that has saved 15 million people from this horrible disease. Interestingly, St Stephen's Green in Dublin was once a leper hospital, and the disease lives on in Irish place names such as Leopardstown.

'I'M GOING DOWN THE SUEZ'

For nearly 150 years, the Suez Canal has played a vital role both in world trade and in giving the nations of the Middle East something else to fight over.
It opened today, in 1869, after a ten-year construction project overseen by Frenchman Ferdinand de Lesseps. But that effort wouldn't have been possible without Francis Chesney from Annalong, Co. Down. It was Chesney who, in 1830, compiled and submitted the report that showed the feasibility of the project. And when Lesseps greeted him in Paris in 1869, he was gracious enough to recognise his debt, calling Chesney the 'Father of the Suez Canal'. Unlike the Panama Canal, the Suez has no locks.

PAT AND MOUSE

Steamboat Willie is famed as the film that introduced Mickey Mouse to the world and started Walt Disney on his rise to fame. The film (released today in 1928) was also one of the first cartoons with synchronised sound, and that is thanks to Pat Powers from Co. Waterford. This movie mogul sold Walt Disney the Cinephone system, which enabled sound cartoons to be made (other systems couldn't get the mouse squeaks right). And when no one would distribute Walt's films, Powers released them through his own company. Powers also co-founded Universal Pictures.

TOO LITTLE NOT TOO LATE

He may not have started his career in TV comedy until he was in his 60s, but Jackie Wright from Belfast certainly had the last laugh. He was the bald, diminutive (4ft 11in/76cm) butt of many, many jokes on *The Benny Hill Show*, and made his debut today in 1969. The trademark speeded-up scenes where Hill would rapidly pat Wright's baldy head to loudly dubbed-in smacking sounds were classics for a whole generation of TV watchers.

HE BREATHED NEW LIFE INTO IT

20 The flute is a cool instrument – and not just because of its interesting role in the film *American Pie*. Long before band camp, it was loved by millions thanks to virtuoso performer James Galway, from Belfast. 'The Man with the Golden Flute' took the mostly orchestral instrument and put it right in the spotlight, thanks to his own million selling albums and famous guest appearances, including Roger Waters' The Wall – Live in Berlin concert. Galway was also a major player on *The Lord of the Rings* soundtrack, released today in 2001.

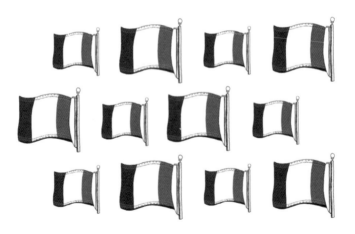

ALL BLACK (AND GREEN)

New Zealand is a country rightly proud of its heritage. And what could be more Kiwi than its rousing national anthem, 'God Defend New Zealand'? Well, something that wasn't written by an Irishman, perhaps. Thomas Bracken from Monaghan wrote the words as a poem in the 1870s, although it was officially adopted as the country's anthem today in 1977. Bracken was also the first person to use the phrase 'God's Own Country' about New Zealand.

NEVER SAY NAVAN AGAIN

Where would the world be without Pierce Brosnan? If it wasn't for the man from Navan, Co. Meath, James Bond might very well be dead and the world would be in the hands of megalomaniacs by now. The film series was in poor shape by the end of the Roger Moore days and in 1986 Brosnan was asked to save the day – alas, he was under contract to play Remington Steele. But he finally got his first mission in 1995 with *Goldeneye* (premièred in London today) – it was the most popular Bond film for decades and rejuvenated the series.

LET THERE BE LIGHT

St Dubhán only wanted a spot of peace and quiet. But no sooner had he founded his lonely cell on Hook Head, Co. Wexford, in the 5th century, than travellers started using his fire as a beacon, and insisting he keep it lit. And so was established Hook Lighthouse, the oldest in the world. The current structure has stood for 800 years, although it has been modernised – electric light replaced paraffin in 1972 and a radar beacon was added today in 1974. While schoolchildren have been throwing paper aeroplanes off the top for decades.

AVANT AVANT-GARDE

No Joyce, no Woolf, no Rushdie – without *Tristram Shandy* there would be no modern novel. Written by Laurence Sterne from Clonmel, Co. Tipperary (born today in 1713), this stunningly original book was centuries ahead of its time. The structure is anarchic, with Tristram not even born until the third volume. There are sermons and legal documents in the text, typography is pushed to the limits, there are marbled pages and a completely black one. No wonder it's mixed up – Sterne fell into a millrace in Annamore, aged seven, and did a full turn round the waterwheel before being rescued.

DO THEY KNOW IT'S FOOKIN' CHRISTMAS?

25 Bob Geldof was so incensed by news images of the African famine that he promptly wrote charity single 'Do They Know It's Christmas?' with Midge Ure. They gathered some pop pals together and recorded it as Band Aid today in 1984. Geldof hoped it might raise £70,000; it became the biggest-selling single in UK chart history, shifting 3.5 million copies and raising millions of pounds. The following summer Geldof's Live Aid concert raised even more millions for charity, and established a new era of fundraising concerts.

HE HAD A VOLCANIC TEMPER

26 Scientists say that the 40,000 hexagonal stone columns are the result of erupted lava cooling around 60 million years ago. But everyone else knows that the Giant's Causeway is part of a bridge built by the Irish titan Fionn mac Cumhaill so he could fight his Scottish counterpart Benandonner. Two million visitors per year come to check out the remains of the world's first ogre-built international highway, and today in 1986 it became a UNESCO World heritage site.

COVENTRY, CO. MAYO

In 1880, English landlords were setting extortionate rents for their Irish tenant farmers. Not even a bad harvest could convince them to show a little leniency. The farmers banded together into the Irish Land League, a movement that soon gained massive popularity. Their first target was a particularly unsympathetic land agent in Co. Mayo, and the local residents all refused to sell him goods, work in his fields, deliver his post or indeed speak to the man. The agent's will broke and he bolted for home on this day. His name was Charles Boycott and we'd given the world an effective new campaigning tactic.

STAR STUDENT

The regular radio pulse coming from space sounded so like a beacon that astrophysics student Jocelyn Bell Burnell dubbed it 'LGM-1' (Little Green Men) when she detected it today in 1967. Actually, it turned out to be a pulsar – a rapidly spinning and very dense star). This helped confirm part of Einstein's theory of general relativity and has been hailed as the greatest astronomical discovery of the 20th century. Belfast-born Burnell achieved it with a 4 acre (1.6ha) radio telescope that she built and operated herself.

DIVINE INSPIRATION

29 *The Book of Kells* is one of the most famous books in the world, a masterwork of calligraphy and beautiful illuminations. The manuscript contains the four Gospels in Latin, and was written in a monastery on Iona around AD 800. But when the Vikings turned up the monks wisely bottled it and fled for the safety of Ireland, taking the book with them. It survived the centuries and was presented to Trinity College, Dublin, in 1661. This national treasure attracts over 500,000 visitors a year and today in 2012, its beauties became digitally available worldwide on an app.

'I'M AN ATHEIST, THANK GOD'

30 David O'Mahony from Firhouse, Dublin, made a huge name for himself as the most controversial comedian of his day – Dave Allen. Politicians and the church were his main targets and his risqué routines included a sketch where the Pope and his cardinals did a musical striptease on the steps of St Peter's. In 1977, RTÉ banned him outright. Today in 1996, he was awarded a lifetime achievement award. Allen put his love of church baiting down to his strict Catholic education – well, being belted by nuns.

DECEMBER

THE GOLDEN BOY

 Ronnie Delany was just 21 when he breasted the tape to beat home favourite John Landy and win the Olympic 1500m gold medal in Melbourne, today in 1956. He set a new Olympic record, and his Olympic victory remains one of the greatest of Irish sporting achievements. But Delany's brilliant career also included an unbroken string of 40 indoor victories and several indoor world records. He is Ireland's most recognisable Olympian as well as one of the greatest sportsmen and international ambassadors in his country's history.

UNSUNG HERO

2 You may not have heard of Omagh songsmith Jimmy Kennedy, but we can guarantee you've danced badly to one of his tunes. Before Lennon and McCartney rocked up, Jimmy had written more hit songs than anyone else in the world. He penned 2,000 songs over a 50-year career. So which one have we all goofed about to? The 'Hokey Cokey', which he wrote today in 1942. And you've probably also gone down to the woods with him – he penned 'The Teddy Bear's Picnic'.

DECEMBER

CAMÁN HAVE A GO IF YOU THINK YOU'RE HARD ENOUGH

With the sliotar topping 93mph (150km/h) from a good strike, hurling is the fastest game on grass. And the game is old, not old like tennis, old as in Before Christ. It was first played here at least 3,000 years ago, and first crops up in print in statutes banning its mayhem today, in 1366. Ancient chroniclers report violent days-long matches between whole towns, but these might simply have been battles. There's not a whole lot of difference if you think about it.

THE WIND OF CHANGE

It's fair to say that snooker was a pretty po-faced sport before Alex 'Hurricane' Higgins roared onto the scene. Chain-smoking, often pissed, always entertaining, people came just to see what the hell he would do next. As a young lad from Belfast he failed in his first career as a jockey because he drank too much Guinness, but that was no impediment to life on the green baize. Flying round the table he played shots so audacious that even other pros were speechless. Higgins became the youngest winner of the World Championship in his first attempt in 1972, and won 20 other titles, including a legendary victory from 7–0 down against Steve Davis to win the UK Championship, today in 1983.

I'D SHIVER HER TIMBERS

Think the *Pirates of the Caribbean* films are just far-fetched fun? One of the most successful ever pirates was a feisty, red-headed Irish lass called Anne Bonny. Her father moved to the Caribbean to make it as a merchant and Anne fell in with 'Calico Jack' Rackham. They married and led a successful pirate life, but when they were eventually caught after a battle, Bonny's last words to the imprisoned Rackham were that she was 'sorry to see him there, but if he had fought like a Man, he need not have been hang'd like a Dog.' Pregnant, she was granted a stay of execution at her trial today in 1720. Later smuggled to safety in South Carolina, she lived to be a grand old dame of 80.

A CLEAN BREAK

Business in Enniskillen was bad for James Gamble's father, so he took his family to America. Young James set up his own soap business today in 1828. He married a Belfast girl, Elizabeth, whose father suggested James do some business with Elizabeth's sister's husband. This man was a candle-maker – they could share raw materials and bounce ideas off each other. The brother-in-law's name was William Procter, and their partnership would go on to change the way the world washes itself.

STEADFAST JOHN

'The Father of the American Navy' was actually John Barry from Tacumshane, Co. Wexford. Today in 1775, he was made the first Captain in the Continental Navy of a US warship commissioned for service. After the war, he became America's first commissioned naval officer, at the rank of Commodore, receiving his commission from President George Washington in 1797. Barry was once offered £100,000 and command of any frigate in the entire British Navy if he would desert the American Navy. The outraged Captain Barry responded that not all the money in the British treasury or command of its entire fleet could tempt him to desert his adopted country.

BORN HERO

Bartholomew Mosse was a surgeon who was so outraged at conditions for expectant mothers in Dublin hospitals that he set up his own: the Dublin Lying-In Hospital. It moved to the Rotunda building today in 1757, which it still occupies, making it the world's oldest maternity hospital: handy, for a nation with the highest birth rate in Europe. Good old Mosse spent so much of his own cash on the venture he was imprisoned for debt. Happily the eccentric doctor escaped through a window and hid in Wales.

RAIN, EXPLAINED

9 Why do clouds float through the air? It's one of those questions that sounds daft, but the more you think about it... Well, the first person to answer it properly was physicist George Stokes from Co. Sligo. 'Stokes' Law' (published today in 1850) concerns particles moving in fluids and it explains why small water droplets can remain suspended in air as clouds, before reaching a critical size and falling as rain. It also explains why sperm swim as they do, which is probably more useful.

PEACE, MAN

10 In the darkest times a light can shine forth more strongly. Throughout the Troubles John Hume was a voice of reason, using his calm intelligence rather than the gun to suggest a way forward. Eventually he was able to help bring the extremes together to explore a peaceful solution. He won the Nobel Peace Prize (today in 1998), the Gandhi Peace Prize, the Martin Luther King award and in 2010 he was chosen as Ireland's Greatest in a poll on RTÉ. It's a grand choice.

BURNING DESIRE FOR KNOWLEDGE

Not many scientists forward human achievement by being spectacularly wrong, but Galway chemist Richard Kirwan was one of them. A brilliant but eccentric man, he always wore his hat and overcoat indoors, kept a pet eagle and lived on nothing but ham and milk. He was the last champion of phlogiston – an element believed to be in everything combustible. He defended it in an essay published today in 1787. Other chemists, including the Frenchman Lavoisier, thought that a burning substance took oxygen from the air. Lavoisier was so irate at Kirwan's essay that he countered each argument line by line. This rebuttal marked the complete triumph of the new, correct, theory.

ALL HYMNS WISE AND WONDERFUL, MISS FRANCES MADE THEM ALL

School assemblies the world over owe a lot to Cecil Frances Alexander from Dublin. This celebrated hymn-writer composed some of the catchiest and best loved works in that genre. Her book, *Hymns for Little Children* (published today in 1848) contains the bona fide classics *There is a Green Hill Far Away*, *Once in Royal David's City* and *All Things Bright and Beautiful*, the last of which she composed at Markree Castle in Co. Sligo.

SHEAR GENIUS

 Woolly thinking isn't necessarily a bad thing. For Frederick Wolseley, from Kingstown, Co. Dublin, it meant fame and fortune. He sailed for Melbourne aged 17 to become a jackaroo, and it was there that he created the world's first sheep-shearing machine. Patented today in 1884, his invention revolutionised the wool industry, speeding up shearing and producing a more complete fleece. An English lad called Herbert Austin joined the company as an apprentice and helped refine the device. When Austin later returned to England and founded his eponymous car company, he named one of his first models after his inspirational boss – the Wolseley.

DECEMBER

DONEGAL WAS ON TRACK FOR SUCCESS

 It might seem odd now, with all its lines gone, but the County Donegal Railway was once the world's most advanced rail system. There were 121 miles (195km) of track with 21 locomotives, 56 passenger vehicles and 304 goods vehicles. Guided by railway visionary Henry Forbes from 1910 to 1943, the network had one of the world's first railway vehicles powered by an internal combustion engine. It was also, today in 1930, the first system in the world to use diesel railcars, a full four years before the Great Western Railway in England.

SAMUEL DAVIDSON? I'M A BIG FAN

 Samuel Davidson sailed from Belfast to run an Indian tea estate, where he built his own tea drier (patented today, in 1877). Returning home, he founded the huge Sirocco Engineering Works to manufacture his patented machinery, and soon he'd revolutionised the tea trade, bringing much cheaper tea to Ireland and Britain. He refined his invention until he'd perfected the forward-bladed centrifugal fan. This proved invaluable in many industries – Sirocco built the biggest fans in existence for mines and thousands for military uses. In an ironic compliment, all the ships in the German fleet scuttled at Scapa Flow in 1919 were found to be fitted with pre-war Sirocco.

THE CEMENT TENT

Next time you're passing Kilbeggan, Co. Westmeath, take a look at one of the world's strangest, but most ingenious buildings. It's the unique 'jelly mould' whiskey warehouse, built by Irish engineer James Waller. Formed only from arches of canvas covered in cement, it is basically a huge concrete tent. It looks mad, but it's a quick, cheap and easy style of building to put up, and with no internal supports it can be used for everything from henhouses to aircraft hangars. Completed today in 1930, it has recently generated a lot of interest as a future solution to housing issues in Africa.

A WOMAN IN 60 MILLION

When you're born Bridget Wren in Tarmons, Co. Kerry, and you end up as Jeban Zeba, wife of Qazi Musa and Queen of Baluchistan, you know you've had a remarkable life. Bridget left for England to be a nurse, but fell in love with Pakistani politician Qazi Musa at Oxford. They married and settled in his home district of Baluchistan, where she followed him into activist politics. Her fair skin, golden hair, blue eyes and Kerry brogue – and her passion – went down well with locals. She founded Pakistan's first women's association and family planning clinic, and today in 1970 was elected to parliament in its first free election.

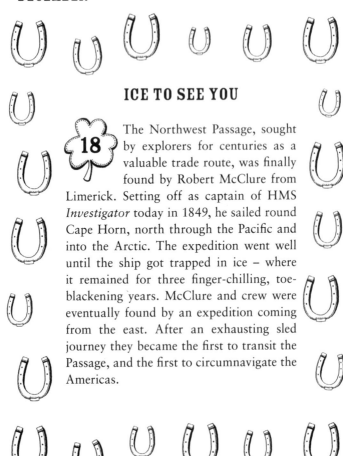

ICE TO SEE YOU

18 The Northwest Passage, sought by explorers for centuries as a valuable trade route, was finally found by Robert McClure from Limerick. Setting off as captain of HMS *Investigator* today in 1849, he sailed round Cape Horn, north through the Pacific and into the Arctic. The expedition went well until the ship got trapped in ice – where it remained for three finger-chilling, toe-blackening years. McClure and crew were eventually found by an expedition coming from the east. After an exhausting sled journey they became the first to transit the Passage, and the first to circumnavigate the Americas.

AND THE BAND DRANK ON

Gaelic Storm are an Irish band who were booked to perform in the film *Titanic* (released today in 1997) as the steerage band, playing the song 'An Irish Party in Third Class'. But when director James Cameron called 'action', he was very unhappy with their performance. The band pointed out that when Cameron had originally seen them play they had been pissed. The director immediately ordered more beer brought on set until they were drunk enough to do a perfect take.

THE SCARLET PIMPERNEL OF THE VATICAN

Oskar Schindler wasn't the only man in the Second World War with a list. Hugh O'Flaherty from Killarney was ordained today in 1925, and posted to the Vatican. Early in the war he visited POW camps and then used Radio Vatican to pass on word of prisoners to their relatives. When Germany occupied Rome in 1943, O'Flaherty and some like-minded friends hid Jews and Allied soldiers from the Nazis. They used convents, farms and even flats beside the SS headquarters. When Rome was liberated, 6,425 of O'Flaherty's escapees were still alive. Monsignor Hugh was also amateur golf champion of Italy.

TOMB IT MAY CONCERN

21 Deep in an ancient hole in the Meath turf, some lucky people will, this morning, be the first to greet the new astronomical year. Newgrange passage tomb is a Neolithic wonder built over 5,000 years ago, long before Stonehenge in England and the Egyptian pyramids. Newgrange is a calendar – at dawn on the winter solstice sunlight illuminates the tomb, announcing the end of the longest night of the year. A few lucky people, chosen by lottery, can watch this from within. Of course, if the skies are overcast, they don't see much. Which is most years, frankly.

THERE WAS A YOUNG MAN FROM...

22 This island has inspired more than its fair share of sublime poems – and we can also lay claim to hordes of the dirtiest, too. Not for nothing is the classic form of rude verse named after Limerick. Of course, you can write a clean limerick, but what would be the point? The cheeky verse was perfected by a bunch called the Maigue Poets, who liked nothing better than to loaf about Croom Castle amusing each other with ditties about a man from Nantucket. It finally reached a wider audience today in 1845, with the publication of Edward Lear's *A Book of Nonsense*.

BECAUSE SICK CATS DON'T CARE WHAT GENDER YOU ARE

The first woman vet in the UK or Ireland was Aleen Cust from Tipperary. She completed her veterinary studies at Edinburgh University in 1897, but was barred from sitting her final exam. Obviously. So she moved to Co. Roscommon, where she simply ignored what the university had said, and joined an understanding practice: one that had lots of forward-thinking animals, presumably. It wasn't until the repeal of the Sex Discrimination Act, today in 1919, that she could be officially recognised by the Royal College of Veterinary Surgeons. Not that Aleen gave a monkey's.

HAPPY CHRISTMAS YOUR ARSE

Shane MacGowan might have been born in England, but just look at the state of the man – he's as Irish as they come. As singer with The Pogues he brought Irish-influenced punk-folk to a worldwide audience. He also wrote what is obviously the best Christmas song of all time (no, not 'Away In A Manger') – 'Fairytale of New York'. This song is famously set on Christmas Eve, babe, in the drunk tank.

GARDEN OF INSPIRATION

Myrtle Grove, the beautiful Tudor house in Youghal, is said to be where Walter Raleigh planted the first potato in Ireland AND where he had a bucket of water thrown over him as he smoked Europe's first ever pipe of tobacco. These tales may be just that, but it is certainly the place where Raleigh became the first person to hear the end of the great poem *The Faerie Queene*. Its author Edmund Spenser lived nearby and finished his epic work in Raleigh's garden. Spenser had been inspired to such brilliance that he was given a pension of £50 a year for life, today in 1591.

PUB PROLIFERATION

You might think there are a lot of pubs in Temple Bar nowadays, but that's nothing compared with how it was in the 17th century. For then the city probably had more hostelries than any other settlement on the planet. In 1610 the author Barnaby Rich said 'It is as rare a thing to find a house in Dublin without a tavern as it is to find a tavern without a strumpet.' And when the Licensing Act of 1635 was passed today, there were 1,180 pubs in Dublin for the 4,000 families who inhabited the place.

DRAMA BEHIND THE SCENES

 Since the curtain was first lifted on its stage today in 1904, The Abbey Theatre in Dublin has been at the cutting edge of world drama. The talents of Sean O'Casey, WB Yeats and John Millington Synge were all nurtured at Ireland's National Theatre. From the start the Abbey drew crowds and controversy – Synge's drama *The Playboy of the Western World* caused a riot on its opening night. The Abbey was also the first state-subsidised theatre in the English-speaking world, which it has enjoyed since 1925.

THIS SONG SHALL BE OUR PARTING HYMN

 'The Red Flag' is the anthem of socialists and protest singers around the world, and it was written by Irishman Jim Connell. A docker and journalist, he wrote the song today in 1889 on the train journey back to his home in Honor Oak, south-east London, from a meeting during the London Dock Strike. Fittingly, the strike was a great success, establishing trade unions in London and inspiring the labour movement. Jim's lyrical inspiration came from the train guard raising and lowering the red signal flag on the platform.

WILL LIGHTNING STRIKE TWICE?

If you're wondering where on earth you can find a huge Corinthian column to climb up inside, the answer is Carrigadaggan Hill, Co. Wexford: for here stands the 95ft (29m) Browne-Clayton monument, the only climbable pillar of its type in the world. Today, in 1994, it was spectacularly struck by lightning, which blew out several stones and left a 16½ft (5m) hole near the top. After repairing it, the builders took wise precautions to prevent such a misfortune happening again – they put a sheaf of corn on top as an offering to the Norse storm god, Woden.

BARNARDO BUILDS A BETTER WORLD

The sheer number of homeless children on the streets of London shocked medical student Thomas Barnardo from Dublin. So he gave up his career and dedicated his life to feeding, housing and educating youngsters. Barnardo opened his first home today in 1870; above its door was a sign, 'No Destitute Boy Ever Refused Admission'. By the time of his death in 1905, he had established 112 district homes, and helped nearly 100,000 children.

INTRODUCING THE G-PLAN DIET

 Maybe good things do come to those who wait – it was the last day of 1759 when Arthur Guinness signed a 9,000-year lease at £45 per annum for a disused brewery in the St James's area of Dublin. Quite apart from anything else, that has to be the single best property-deal in Irish history. But it was also the birth of the legendary black stuff. Not that Guinness is black, of course; it is actually very, very dark red. And despite its reputation as a 'meal in a glass', a pint of plain only has 198 calories, less than skimmed milk. So why not put some on your cornflakes for a fitting end to a great Irish year…

Sláinte!

Ireland sober is Ireland stiff.

JAMES JOYCE

ACKNOWLEDGEMENTS

I'd like to send the hugest of thanks out to Bill Walsh for ideas, travel tips and directions to Belfast's best boozers.

Thanks also to Megan White, Pat Daly, Aisling Cusack and Jennifer Quinn for telling me what makes them so proud of their island.

This book wouldn't have been possible without The National Museum of Ireland (Archaeology and Decorative Arts & History), The Natural History Museum (Ireland), The Ulster Museum, The Ulster Folk & Transport Museum, Titanic's Dock & Pump House and The Little Museum of Dublin.

ALSO AVAILABLE FROM PORTICO

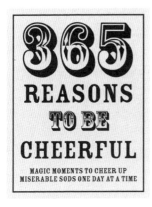

Richard Happer
Hardback • £7.99
9781906032968

Richard Happer
Hardback • £7.99
9781907554681

This joy-filled book contains a whole year's worth of funny and unique events that happened on each and every day – a wild, weird and wonderful journey through the year, highlighting moments that changed the world for the better and delightful, irreverent stories that are guaranteed to put a smile on your face.

365 Reasons to Look on the Bright Side is full of stories of good fortune arisen out of the flames of errors, blunders and miscalculations, with a happy ending for every day of the year. A perfect present for miserable pessimists as well as eternal optimists, it shows that it really is true that every cloud has a silver lining!

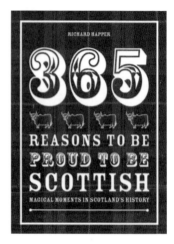

Richard Happer
Hardback • £7.99
9781907554391

Richard Happer
Hardback • £7.99
9781907554872

Has there ever been a more inventive, adventurous, creative and eccentric race than the British? We don't think so, and *365 Reasons to be Proud to be British* proves it brilliantly. In this book you'll find a year's worth of the discoveries, delights and derring-do that make Britain a place of wonder.

365 Reasons to be Proud to be Scottish is a year-long romp of jolliness taking in the quirky events, inventions, traditions, people, places and characters that make Scotland a country worth celebrating every day of the year, from magical monster myths to the ancient Highland whisky makers.

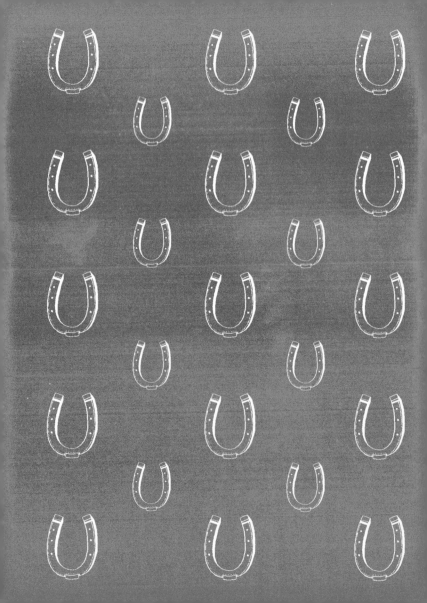